Claudia and the Genius of Elm Street

THE BABY-SITTERS CLUB
titles in Large-Print Editions:

Claudia and the Genius of Elm Street
Ann M. Martin

Gareth Stevens Publishing
MILWAUKEE

For a free color catalog describing Gareth Stevens' list of high-quality books
and multimedia programs, call 1-800-542-2595 (USA) or 1-800-461-9120 (Canada).
Gareth Stevens Publishing's Fax: (414) 225-0377.
See our catalog, too, on the World Wide Web: http://gsinc.com

Library of Congress Cataloging-in-Publication Data

Martin, Ann M., 1955-
    Claudia and the genius of Elm Street / by Ann M. Martin.
        p.   cm. -- (The Baby-sitters Club; #49)
    Summary: Claudia, the most artistic member of the Baby-sitters Club, has her hands
full working on an art project and babysitting for a seven-year-old genius.
    ISBN 0-8368-1573-4 (lib. bdg.)
    [1. Babysitters--Fiction. 2. Clubs--Fiction. 3. Genius--Fiction. 4. Artists--Fiction.]
I. Title. II. Series: Martin, Ann M., 1955- Baby-sitters Club; #49.
PZ7.M3567585Clge 1996
[Fic]--dc20   96-15708

Published by Gareth Stevens, Inc., 1555 North RiverCenter Drive, Suite 201, Milwaukee,
Wisconsin 53212 in large print by arrangement with Scholastic Inc., 555 Broadway, New York,
New York 10012.

Cover art by Hodges Soileau.

Printed in the United States of America

1 2 3 4 5 6 7 8 9 99 98 97 96

*The author gratefully acknowledges
Peter Lerangis
for his help in
preparing this manuscript.*

CHAPTER 1

"**H**oney, watch where you're going with that. Don't spill it on the — who-o-o-oa!"

It was a Friday afternoon, and I was staring at the TV, bored stiff with this commercial that had come on for about the twentieth time. In it, some girl spills a huge glass of chocolate milk on a living room carpet (white, of course). Her mom gets hysterical, then sprays the stain with some carpet cleaner. Out of the can rushes a team of hungry cartoon gremlins. Ta-da! The gremlins eat the stain and the mom hugs the girl, who smiles cutely with one front tooth missing. Happy music plays in the background.

So realistic. I mean, does anyone ask how the gremlins got *in* the spray can? Wouldn't the mom and daughter run away screaming if they really saw those disgusting things? And what happens to the gremlins after they fin-

1

ish? Do they hang out in the house forever? Ew.

All I wanted to do was watch this documentary about the artist Andy Warhol. (I'm really into art, and I figured the show might inspire me.)

I know what you're thinking. I should have taped the show so I could zap through the commercials. Well, I *did* tape it. Or at least I thought I did.

It wasn't until 4:10 on Friday afternoon that I realized I'd goofed. There I was, walking through our living room. My sister, Janine the genius, was reading the newspaper. She looked up at me and said, "You know, that special you wanted to watch already started — "

"I know," I said, nodding confidently. "I'm taping it — "

That's when I looked at the VCR and saw that it wasn't lit up. I quickly turned it on and saw 1:00:00 on the display, which meant I'd already taped an hour of *something*.

"What happened?" Janine said.

"I don't know," I answered. I rewound part of the tape and played it. It was this weird movie about aliens attacking a hippie commune or something. "I programmed it from four to five, but — "

"A.M. or P.M.?" Janine asked innocently.

2

Duh.

There I stood, Claudia Kishi, the Dunce of the Kishi family. I had taped the Late Late *Late* Show.

Which is why I ended up watching the Andy Warhol documentary right then and there, complete with commercials.

It was worth it, though. At least *I* thought so. Warhol would paint an ordinary object, like a Campbell's soup can, in a way that made you want to *look* at it — as if it were the most interesting thing in the world. He also made wild-colored silkscreen portraits of legendary movie stars, like Marilyn Monroe and James Dean and Elvis Presley.

Well, Janine sat through about thirty seconds of this before she announced, "I don't understand how you can call that stuff *art*." Then she walked off, probably to study advanced calculus or physics or something else just as fun-filled.

Janine is only a junior in high school, but they ran out of classes hard enough for her, so she's taking courses at a local college. Me? I'm thirteen, and in eighth grade at Stoneybrook Middle School, in Stoneybrook, Connecticut. I have a hard enough time with normal classes. The first time I heard Janine mention "calculus" I thought she was talking about a Roman emperor. Then she showed

3

me her book. You know what the strangest thing was? Calculus is supposed to be a kind of *math* — but there were hardly any numbers! It was mostly a bunch of squiggles and letters. Janine tried to explain it to me, but I suddenly felt like I'd taken a sleeping pill. *Boring!*

As you can gather, my sister and I could hardly be more different. We *do* both have dark hair and almond-shaped eyes (our family is Japanese-American), but that's about it. I'm into wild clothes and different hairstyles. That afternoon, for instance, I was wearing a man's paisley vest I'd found at a yard sale, over a striped button-down shirt with tuxedo-stripe black Spandex stirrup pants, held up with pink-flecked black suspenders. My hair was pulled straight back with a paisley comb, and I was wearing electric-pink ankle boots. The boots really set off the formality of the rest of the outfit, sort of like the punchline of a joke. I think you can tell a lot about people from the way they dress. If you saw me, you might think: *artistic, fun-loving, good sense of humor.* At least I hope you'd think that.

If you saw Janine, you'd think: *smart, very smart, unbelievably smart.* Her hair is always in a page boy, and she'd be perfectly happy wearing a white Oxford blouse and a gray pleated skirt every day. Janine's main accessory is a book cradled in her right arm. Exactly

4

the way you'd expect someone with a 196 I.Q. to dress.

That's right, 196. "Normal" is 100, "bright" is 120, and "genius" is 150. So what does that make Janine? It scares me just to think of it.

I used to be kind of resentful of my sister. I thought she could do no wrong in my parents' eyes. (My dad's an investment banker and my mom's a librarian, so they're both into Achievement and Applying Yourself.) For a long time only my grandmother Mimi understood my interests. Mimi lived with us, but when she died I felt so . . . *alone* in my family. Now things have changed. Janine and I get along pretty well, and my parents are beginning to realize that I'm serious about my art (and good at it). And since Mimi's gone, I have a picture of her on my bedroom wall for inspiration. Actually it's a photo of Mimi when she was my age, and it's amazing how much she looks like me.

Somehow I can't imagine that Mimi ever had a room like mine, though. It's . . . well, *multipurpose*. For one thing, it's the place where I sleep. (No kidding.) For another, it's my studio. I have supplies stashed everywhere — brushes, palettes, an easel, paints, charcoal pencils, plaster of paris, old newspapers for papier-mâché, and a box of small beads and objects for jewelry making. My walls might as well be called "the Claudia Kishi gallery."

That's what you notice the moment you walk into my room. What you *don't* notice is all the hidden stuff — junk food and Nancy Drew mysteries! Those are my secret passions. They're stuffed under my mattress, tucked away in corners and drawers, folded into sweaters in my closet. Why? Well, my parents don't approve of junk food, and they don't like the Nancy Drew books because they think I should be reading "literature." Actually I have nothing against literature. I liked *The Lion, the Witch and the Wardrobe*. I even liked *Oliver Twist*, despite the fact that it took *forever* to read (and weighed about a hundred pounds). But to me, reading is kind of like food. You can't eat filet mignon all the time. It's nice to have some ice cream and cake. Nancy Drew mysteries are my ice cream and cake.

Oh, I should mention something before you think I'm a complete pig — I give away a lot of my junk food. You see, my room is also the official meeting place for a club my friends and I belong to, the Baby-sitters Club. And there's nothing like having Doritos or Snickers bars or M&M's to pass around when you're waiting for business. I'll tell you more about the BSC later.

Back to Andy Warhol. As I mentioned, I was

watching the show for inspiration. I had been feeling a little bored and empty, like something about my artwork was missing. Not that I wasn't busy. I've always spent my spare time doodling, painting, making jewelry, making collages, sculpting . . . but that's what was wrong. I felt like I was doing *too* much, and not really digging into anything.

I needed a new project, something I could spend time on and be proud of.

So there were Andy Warhol's paintings: cans of Campbell's soup and Del Monte peaches, bottles of Heinz ketchup, boxes of Brillo soap pads . . .

Suddenly I sat up. Can you picture those old cartoons in which a character gets an idea, and you hear a BOIING! and see a lightbulb above his head? Well, that's how I felt.

All I could think about were Milky Way bars and Ring Dings and Oreos. No, I wasn't hungry. Not at all.

Those things were going to be the subjects of my next art project! I could see it so clearly — a series of pop art pieces, "Junk Food Fantasy," by Claudia Kishi. I could paint a Twinkie in a wrapper, then a Twinkie unwrapped. A Yankee Doodle, and then a Yankee Doodle with a bite in it. All in realistic detail with vivid colors.

The idea was brilliant (not to mention that

it would give me an excuse to buy even more junk food). I couldn't wait to get started. I turned off the show before it was over and ran upstairs to my room.

I began a few preliminary sketches, but two things happened. One, I got hungry and ate the subject of my fifth sketch, a Chunky bar. Two, I realized it was getting close to five-thirty. And five-thirty on a Friday meant just one thing — a BSC meeting.

I began to clean up my room. I was dying to tell my friends about my great new idea.

CHAPTER 2

How does light play off the curves of a Fritos corn chip?

How do you create detail in a white Yankee Doodle center?

Which is more interesting, the many textures of a Snickers bar or the simplicity of a Three Musketeers bar?

These were the incredibly important questions in my head as I cleaned up. That's the thing about art. You get obsessed about the weirdest details. How should the object be lit — from behind, from above, from the right, or from the left? Should your green have more blue in it or more yellow? Should your whites be pure or tinted toward gray — or toward brown? How big should the subject be? What should be in the background?

I find stuff like that fascinating. A lot of people would find it more interesting to talk about brussels sprouts.

I was so deep in thought I didn't even hear Kristy Thomas walk into my room around five-fifteen. (Kristy's the BSC president.) "Hey, Claud," she said.

"Oh! Hi," I answered.

I must have looked like I was in another world, because Kristy stopped and stared at me. "What's wrong?" she asked.

I was about to ask her what she thought about the Snickers–Three Musketeers issue, but I caught myself. She'd probably think I was out of my mind. Instead I said, "Just thinking about a new art project."

Kristy's eyes lit up. She's always interested in new ideas and challenges. "Really? What?"

"Well . . . I'm going to work on a series of realistic junk-food portraits. Sort of like Andy Warhol."

You should have seen Kristy's face. It went totally blank. "Uh-huh," she said, looking around the room. "Great."

Whoops. It's not that Kristy is a Philistine (that's a word Janine taught me — it means "one who is ignorant of artistic things"). She always has smart things to say about my work. It's just that her idea of a *good idea* is much more . . . practical. Kristy's the type of person who will take an impossible problem and figure out how to solve it. Here's an example: Kristy's younger brothers and sister wanted to play on a softball team, but they weren't ready for Little League. So what did Kristy do? She formed a team by herself, called Kristy's Krushers.

From the way Kristy dresses, you'd think she was on her way to a softball game every day. She always looks good, just very casual — jeans, a T-shirt or turtleneck, and running shoes. Her face is friendly, with pretty brown eyes and long brown hair. She's on the short side and very athletic.

Kristy is the perfect club president. She has the loudest voice (which helps in a group of talkers like us). She's not afraid to say what's on her mind, and she'll boss people around if she has to. Some people are bothered by her bluntness, but we all accept it. She's just . . . Kristy.

I should know. We've been friends since we were in diapers. The Thomases used to live across the street from me. Back in the old days, the Thomas family was pretty ordinary. It consisted of Kristy, her mom and dad, and her two older brothers, Sam and Charlie. Then, when Kristy was about six, Mr. Thomas just walked out on them. Why? No one knows for sure, but I think it was a rotten thing to do. Kristy's younger brother, David Michael, had just been born, and all of a sudden Mrs. Thomas had to support four kids. Somehow

11

she managed to juggle a job, childcare, shopping, you name it (I guess that's where Kristy gets her organizational skills).

Everything changed for Kristy's family not long ago. Mrs. Thomas met this millionaire named Watson Brewer. They fell madly in love and got married, and the Thomases ended up moving into a huge mansion. And let me tell you, that house *needs* to be huge. Watson is the divorced father of two kids, Karen and Andrew, who spend every other weekend and some vacations and holidays at the house. Then there's Emily Michelle, an adorable two-and-a-half-year-old Vietnamese girl whom Watson and Kristy's mother recently adopted. Then there's Nannie, Kristy's grandmother on her mom's side, who now lives there and helps take care of Emily Michelle. And then there are Boo-Boo and Shannon, a cat and a dog.

Needless to say, her house is a pretty wild place. It's also on the other side of town, but of course Kristy's worked that out, too. Her brother Charlie drives her back here for BSC meetings.

And she's *always* the first one to arrive.

Take that Friday after the TV show. Ten minutes before anyone else came, there was Kristy, busily helping me clean up. Did I mind? No way.

Before long, Dawn and Mary Anne showed up, then Mallory and Jessi. Stacey arrived last, at 5:28.

That's the whole club. They are my closest friends in the world, and they're all so different. Let me tell you about them.

My best friend in the BSC (and in life) is Stacey McGill. We have a lot in common, starting with our sense of style. I'd say we are both sophisticated, but that sounds stuck-up (oh well, I said it anyway). Stacey is clothes-conscious like me, but in a more *urban* way — very chic and glamorous. Stacey is blonde and gorgeous, and she's from New York City. For a while she moved back to New York when her father's company transferred him there. Whoa, did I miss her! But then her parents divorced, and Stacey decided to return to Stoneybrook with her mother. I was thrilled she came back, but sad about her parents splitting up. Stacey's still close with both of them. She visits her dad pretty often.

Here's the main difference between Stacey and me. If you asked us both a math question, I'd probably make you repeat it, then sit there trying to write it all out, then start doodling. Stacey would figure it out in her head. When it comes to math, I think she's in Janine's league.

Oh, one other thing we don't have in common. Stacey doesn't eat sweets. It's not because she doesn't like them, it's because she has diabetes. That means she has to be careful about sugar. If she eats too much (or too little), she can get really sick. There's a reason for it, something about not having a certain chemical in her bloodstream. (One of these days I'll understand it, but biology is not my strong point.) Every day she has to give herself injections of something called insulin. I'm glad I don't have to watch. I'd probably faint.

And Mary Anne Spier would probably plop right down next to me. She is Ms. Sensitive. Forget about inviting her over to watch a sad movie. You'll run out of Kleenex. I found that out one day when we saw a tape of *E.T.* together. You know the scene where the kids are smuggling E.T. away on their bikes, and they take off into the air? That scene makes me stand up and cheer. But Mary Anne bursts into tears. When I asked her why, she said, "I'm so . . . *happy* for them!"

As you can probably tell, Mary Anne is a very caring person and a great friend. She's shy, too, and a little conservative, but she's getting more and more stylish. That afternoon, for example, she wore a loose-fitting open shirt over a teal turtleneck with off-white chinos and white sneakers.

I think it's funny that the two BSC members who are opposites — quiet Mary Anne and loud Kristy — are best friends. They do look similar, though. Like Kristy, Mary Anne has long brown hair, brown eyes, and friendly features.

I think it's also funny that the shyest one of us has the only long-term boyfriend. His name is Logan Bruno, and he's an associate BSC member (our other associate member is named Shannon Kilbourne). Mary Anne and Logan have been together for a long time, and they've even survived a breakup.

Fortunately, by the time they met, Mary Anne had stopped fixing her hair in braids and wearing babyish clothing. I hate to say it, but poor Mary Anne used to look positively prehistoric. Not that she *wanted* to. It was just that her dad was very strict about her appearance. You see, he had to raise Mary Anne by himself because Mrs. Spier died when Mary Anne was a baby. Don't get me wrong, Mr. Spier's a nice man — but he went overboard sometimes. Mary Anne's life was rules, rules, rules. Things have loosened up a lot, though, because her dad remarried. And, believe it or not, his new wife just happens to be the mother of . . .

Dawn Schafer, another member of our club!

Dawn is the club's other blonde, a "California girl." She's laid-back and wears fun, colorful, casual clothes. She's a vegetarian, and she loves health food. Her idea of a snack is roasted corn nuts or bean sprouts-and-tofu sandwiches on pita bread with organic mayonnaise. I mean it. In our meetings, when the smell of chocolate would be enough to make anyone drool, Dawn is perfectly happy with a whole-wheat cracker.

Dawn was born and raised practically walking distance from Disneyland. But when her parents divorced, her mom moved Dawn and her younger brother, Jeff, to Stoneybrook. Mrs. Schafer grew up here and I guess she missed her old town. Then, after a short time in Connecticut, Jeff decided *he* missed California, and Mrs. Schafer let him move back with his dad (that was a pretty stormy time in the Schafer house). Dawn was awfully sad when Jeff left.

Anyway, Mrs. Schafer soon got together with one of her old boyfriends from Stoneybrook High. His name was Richard Spier! That's right, Dawn's mom and Mary Anne's dad used to date in high school. When they met each other after all those years, they fell madly in love again and got married.

Mary Anne and her father moved to the

Schafers', this big old farmhouse on Burnt Hill Road. It was built in the 1700s, and Dawn thinks it's haunted. It's full of creaky floorboards and windows that whistle in the wind. But the best part is a secret underground passage that leads from the barn to . . . Dawn's bedroom! Dawn is convinced that a ghost lives in the passage. She *insists* it's true. (You want to know what I think? I think she spent too much time at the haunted mansion in Disneyland when she was a kid.) Frankly, though, I have no idea how she manages to sleep at night.

Next are Jessi and Mal — that is, Jessica Ramsey and Mallory Pike. They're in sixth grade, two grades behind the rest of us. Both of them are really talented and great babysitters. Jessi dances like a pro. She studies ballet, and it really shows. She even carries herself like a dancer — her back straight, her feet turned out, her ankles usually covered with leg warmers.

Becca and Squirt are Jessi's younger sister and brother. *Becca* is short for Rebecca (she's nine) and *Squirt* is a nickname, too (Jessi's brother's real name is John Philip Ramsey, Jr.). Squirt is only a baby now, but I wonder if he'll use his nickname when he gets older.

One other thing about Jessi. She's the only

black member of the BSC. That's because the Ramseys are one of the very few black families in Stoneybrook. When they first moved here, some people gave them a rough time. But things are much smoother now. As far as us BSC members are concerned, that prejudice was absolutely stupid.

I think Mallory Pike may secretly like being one of our younger members. That's because in real life she's the oldest of — get ready — eight kids. Can you imagine? Her brothers and sisters are Vanessa, Margo, Nicky, the triplets (Adam, Jordan, and Byron), and Claire. No wonder Mal's favorite pastimes are writing and drawing. They're things she can do *alone*. Mal's dream in life, by the way, is to be a children's book author and illustrator.

Anyway, there they are, the Baby-sitters Club in person. (Or is it "in persons"? "In people"?) That Friday's meeting started out typically. We were noisy and excited (it *was* the start of the weekend, after all). I was explaining my project to the others. For some reason, it seemed to make everyone twice as hungry. The Milky Ways and M&M's were going like crazy (not to mention the pretzels for Dawn and Stacey).

Kristy was sitting in her official place, a director's chair by my desk. She was wearing her visor, and a pencil was tucked over one ear. Her eyes were glued to the digital clock on my dresser, which read 5:29. At *precisely* five-thirty she called out, "Order!"

The Baby-sitters Club meeting had officially begun.

CHAPTER 3

We were all in position. Mary Anne, Stacey, and I were cross-legged on my bed. Dawn had turned my desk chair around and was sitting in it with her arms resting on the back. Mal and Jessi were stretched out on the carpet.

"Any new business?" Kristy asked.

The answer to Kristy's question was the sound of jaws chomping. Everyone looked around silently.

"Guess not," Kristy said.

I noticed that Kristy and I were the only ones not eating. I reached into my night-table drawer, remembering a Kit-Kat I had hidden once. Sure enough, it was still there. I broke it in half and offered one of the pieces to Kristy.

"Save that half," Kristy said. "You can make a painting of it."

"Good idea," I said. But that wasn't how I *felt*. You know how hard it is to *not* eat the

20

other half of a candy bar? All I wanted to do was gulp it down.

I looked at it longingly. Maybe this project wasn't such a smart idea.

I decided to concentrate on the phone, which was right next to me. If I looked at it hard enough, it just might start to ring.

My phone, by the way, is the reason we use my room for BSC meetings. I'm the only club member who has her own private line. And the Baby-sitters Club couldn't be the Baby-sitters Club without a phone.

Here's how the BSC works. We meet from 5:30 to 6:00 every Monday, Wednesday, and Friday afternoon. Our clients (neighborhood parents) call us during those times, asking for a baby-sitter for such and such a day. We check each member's schedule, then figure out who can cover the job. Someone is usually available — and if no one is, Logan and Shannon are our backups. With just one phone call, each client is assured of a reliable, experienced sitter.

Simple, right? It's really a great idea, and I'll bet you can guess who thought of it.

If you guessed Kristy, you were right. It all started one day when Kristy's mom needed someone to sit for David Michael (this was before she was married to Watson). She ended up making about a million phone calls, and no one was available. Kristy felt really bad for her. She wished there were some easier way to find a sitter. She began to think: Suppose you needed a taxi or an ambulance or a police officer? You wouldn't have to call each car separately to find a free one. You'd call a central number and . . .

BOIING! The lightbulb went on above Kristy's head. She called me and Mary Anne and suggested the idea of the Baby-sitters Club. We agreed to try it. I even invited Stacey, whom I had just met, to join. We put an ad in the Stoneybrook newspaper and tacked up fliers around the neighborhood — with my phone number and our meeting times.

Business was great right from the beginning. In fact, it was *so* good that we had to expand. That's where Dawn came in. She had just moved to Stoneybrook, and she was thrilled to join. Then, after Stacey moved to New York, we took on Mal and Jessi. (When Stacey returned we let her right back in, of course.) For good measure, we had added Logan and Shannon as associates.

Our meetings are fun. But, as Kristy says, "We're not only a club, we're a business." Each of us is an officer with special duties. Kristy, as president, runs the meetings. She also makes sure we write down our baby-sitting experiences in the club notebook. That way we can tell each other about new clients, describe how we solved problems, stuff like that. Kristy was the one who thought up the idea of the notebook, and I have to admit it's really helpful. But it's sort of like brushing your teeth — a good thing to do, but not a whole lot of fun. Especially if you have horrible handwriting and can't spell, like me! I always think the other girls are going to laugh at my entries, even though they *say* they never do.

Another one of Kristy's great ideas is Kid-Kits. These are boxes we sometimes take on our jobs. They're filled with simple things kids can play with, like Magic Markers, paper, books, and small toys and games. They're not fancy but they really save the day sometimes. Kids *love* them.

Now, when a call comes in to the BSC, the first person we turn to is Mary Anne. She's our secretary, and she has to keep track of everyone's schedule. This is not easy, considering our club has seven members. You should see the record book she keeps. It's marked off in grids, with color-coded entries in this tiny, neat handwriting. She carefully writes down every one of Jessi's ballet classes, Mallory's orthodontist appointments, my art classes, Kristy's softball games. She also keeps an up-to-date record of client information — names, addresses, phone numbers, special likes and dislikes, allergies, you name it. It's a lot of work, but you know what? Mary Anne never makes mistakes. I don't know how she does it. If I had her job, the club would fold in a week.

And it would fold in a *day* if I had Stacey's job. Stacey, the math whiz, is our treasurer. She keeps track of the club money. No, we don't hand over our earnings to her or anything like that. We get to keep whatever we make. So what does Stacey keep track of? Well, here's the only not-so-fun part about the BSC. We have to pay dues. Every Monday. No one likes to do it, but that's life. The money goes to our "overhead," as Stacey calls it. That means paying Charlie to drive Kristy to and from meetings, keeping the Kid-Kits stocked, and helping to pay my phone bill. If there's ever any leftover cash, we sometimes have a sleepover or a pizza party.

Dawn is our alternate officer. That means she substitutes for anyone who misses a meeting — for sickness, family vacation, baby-sitting appointment, whatever. She was our treasurer for a long time while Stacey was living in New York, but she gladly gave that job back when Stace returned.

Jessi and Mal are our junior officers, since

they're not allowed to baby-sit late at night (unless they're watching their own brothers and sisters). They keep busy, though, sitting on weekend days and afternoons, which frees the rest of us to take nighttime sitting jobs.

Me? I'm the club's vice-president, which mostly means answering the phone during nonclub hours and keeping everyone's sweet tooth satisfied. That's fine with me!

Okay, getting back to Friday. I didn't eat the other half of the Kit-Kat, and it wasn't long before the phone rang.

I picked it up. "Hello, Baby-sitters Club," I said cheerfully.

"Uh, hello dear, Ginger Wilder here," a voice answered. "I got your number from the Barretts."

Ginger Wilder here? That was a strange greeting, I thought. Was I supposed to know who she was or something?

"Right," I said warmly, "we've all sat for the Barrett kids: Buddy, Suzie — "

"And dear little Marnie," Mrs. Wilder said, cutting me off. "Yes, Mrs. Barrett has mentioned that you girls are quite lovely and talented. Now, I'm looking for a sitter on a regular basis. Is this something you handle?"

"Regular?" I repeated. "You mean like a permanent job?"

"Oh, no, no, no," Ginger Wilder said with a chuckle. "You see, my mother has become awfully ill. She's seventy, never been sick a day in her life, and now all of sudden, *bam!* Thursday she tripped and broke her ankle, then she came down with the flu, and now shingles, of all things. She really needs someone to look after her for a few weeks, and my sister and I have worked out a caretaking schedule."

I noticed she pronounced schedule "*shed-yool.*" Up till then, I'd only heard English actors on TV say it that way. And what on earth did she mean by *shingles*?

"My days," she continued, "are Tuesdays, Thursdays, and Fridays. My husband doesn't come home till eight, eight-thirty, so I'll need someone those three evenings to sit for my daughter, Rosie. She's seven."

"I think we can handle it — " I began.

"It will be *frightfully* easy," Mrs. Wilder barged on. "Rosie is quite occupied with her lessons after school. We've found the most marvelous private teachers who come to our house. Makes things very convenient. You know, it's tough enough to manage a daughter's career and be a good mother without having to traipse around town from teacher to teacher. . . . Anyway, I don't mean to chew your ear off. Can you girls help me?"

"I'm sure we can," I said. "Would you please hold for a moment?"

"Of course."

I put my hand over the mouthpiece. Looking up, I noticed everyone staring at me with puzzled expressions. I must have been making faces into the phone. "Is something wrong?" Mary Anne asked.

I shook my head and told them what Mrs. Wilder wanted. (I was dying to describe her in detail, but she might have heard me.)

Mary Anne carefully checked the record book. "Tuesday, Thursday, Friday . . . hmm, well, for the next two weeks *you're* free all but one of those days, Claud," she said.

I took my hand away from the receiver. "You're all set, Mrs. Wilder," I said. "I'll be your sitter."

"Super!" she replied. "You don't happen to have an interest in dance or music, do you?"

"Uh, no . . ." I replied, "but I'm sure — "

"Or science and math?" she asked. "Are you in one of those clubs at school?"

I wanted to laugh, but I didn't. "No. I'm mostly interested in art."

"Oh, an *artist*, a budding Georgia O'Keeffe," Mrs. Wilder said. "Yes, well, Rosie likes to draw a bit when she has a few moments. So!

27

I shall see you on Tuesday, then? Three-thirty on the nose? We live at 477 Elm Street, near Locust Avenue."

"Okay, see you then!" I said.

As soon as I hung up the phone, Stacey gave me a big grin and said, "Lucky*yyyyy* . . ."

"This is great, Claudia," Kristy added. "Three days a week, a new client . . . what was the mother like? She seemed to talk a lot."

"Yeah," I agreed. "She's . . . friendly."

"You should have seen the expression on your face," Jessi said. "You were giving her this *look* . . ."

I smiled. "She has this funny kind of voice. Like actresses in those old black-and-white movies. *Mah*velous, *dah*ling — you know, like that. And she said the strangest thing, something about *managing* her daughter's career."

"Maybe the daughter's like Brooke Shields," Dawn said. "Her mom managed her full-time from when she was a baby."

"I'm sure it'll be fun whatever it is," Kristy said.

"I guess," I replied.

"But it's only temporary?" Mallory asked, looking a little confused. "Is Mrs. Wilder taking a class or something?"

"No, *her* mom's sick," I said. "Rosie's grandmother. A broken ankle, flu — and something to do with . . . *shingles*."

"Ohhhhh," Mary Anne said with a pained expression. "My grandfather had shingles. It's some kind of virus that older people get, and it hurts like crazy. Your body just itches and itches for weeks, and there's nothing you can do about it."

"Ew," I said, but that was as far as I got before the phone rang.

As I reached for it, I remember having this strange feeling. Like something was wrong about this job. Like it wasn't going to be easy at all. Was it something Ginger Wilder had said? Was it the tone of her voice?

Maybe it was the fact that I couldn't picture Rosie. Most of the time when a new client calls, I automatically imagine what the children will be like.

But when I tried to think of Rosie, I came up with a great big blank.

I picked up the ringing phone. "Hello, Babysitters Club."

Oh, well, I'd have to wait for Tuesday to find out what I was in for.

CHAPTER 4

Tuesday, came. I walked to the Wilders' house feeling nervous. I told myself that was normal for meeting a new client.

The Wilders' house was a Cape Cod-style house, off-white with green shutters. A dogwood tree stood to the left of it and neatly cut hedges lined the porch. A maroon station wagon was in the driveway.

Totally normal.

I was *soooo* relieved.

Relieved? What was I expecting? Well, even though I couldn't picture Rosie, I had an image of the Wilder house. It was a mansion with servants. A butler would answer the door and say, "May I escort you to the mistress Rosie's changing room?" And Ginger Wilder would sweep down the staircase with a flowing gown, announcing "I'm off, dear. Ta-ta. Just tell the cook what you'd like for dinner — lobster or steak."

No such luck. I stood before the aluminum screen door and rang a white plastic bell. I could hear a classical piano recording inside. It was pretty loud, and no one was answering the door, so I figured the music had drowned out the bell. I decided to knock.

"Just a minute!" came Mrs. Wilder's voice.

When the door opened, I felt relieved again.

Mrs. Wilder had a pretty, friendly face. Her hair was a beautiful deep brown, pulled straight back with a comb. She was wearing a string of pearls and a blue Laura Ashley dress. Her smile put me at ease. "Welcome, Claudia," she said, shaking my hand. "How nice to meet you. Come in."

"Hi," I said.

I glanced around. I noticed a framed Chagall print on one wall, a Matisse on another. That meant the Wilders probably had an interest in art. Definitely a good sign.

The music grew louder, and the sound was fantastic. You know how it is when you're in a new house. You take everything in and quickly try to figure out what to say first. You find something in the house you can compliment or talk about. I was going to mention the artwork, then say what a great sound system they had, then —

That's when I noticed that the sound system wasn't a sound system.

It was live.

A person was playing the piano in the living room. A girl whose feet barely reached the pedals.

"Rosie!" Mrs. Wilder said.

The girl kept playing. And I mean *playing*. Her fingers were flying over the keys.

Mrs. Wilder walked closer to her daughter. "Rosie?" she repeated.

The girl didn't look up. She was concentrating hard, with this grim expression on her face.

"Mary Rose, I'm talking to you!" Mrs. Wilder said in an annoyed voice.

Finally the girl stopped. She let her hands fall off the piano. "What?"

"Claudia is here," Mrs. Wilder said with a big smile.

"Hi," I said, waving and looking as friendly as I could.

No reaction.

"Claudia's your sitter," Mrs. Wilder said. I wondered if that was the first Rosie had heard about me.

"I know," Rosie said.

Mrs. Wilder's smile was beginning to look forced. "Well, aren't you going to come say hello?"

Rosie slipped off her seat, crossed the room, and shook my hand. She had flaming, thick red hair, a scattering of freckles, and hazel eyes. "Hi," she said. She sounded about as excited as a kid in detention.

"That was really . . . nice," I said.

"It's Mozart," Rosie replied. "Those last few chords weren't supposed to be rolled like that, but my hands aren't quite large enough."

"Uh-huh," I said. I had no idea what she was talking about.

Mrs. Wilder broke into the silence. "Now," she said, "Mrs. Wood usually comes at four o'clock to give a piano lesson, but she has the flu today so Rosie is using this time to practice. Wednesday is her ballet class and her violin lesson — which naturally won't concern you, Claudia — but on Thursday, her voice teacher and tap instructor both come at five-fifteen. Normally it's just her voice teacher, but Rosie has an important dinner-theater audition coming up. Her agent says she needs a solid song-and-dance number under her belt, so we decided both teachers should be present. And, let's see . . . Friday is science club, which meets after school, so you don't have to be here until a quarter to five."

"Wow!" I said. "What a lot of talents."

Ah-ha! A smile! It was faint, but Rosie's lips were turning up slightly.

Mrs. Wilder laughed. "Oh, that's not the half. There's also math club on Mondays and the advanced readers' group at the library every other Saturday. Not to mention our trips to New York for commercial auditions and tapings, modeling calls, agent meetings . . ." She rolled her eyes and wiped her brow. *"Whew!* It's a full-time job. Right, honey?"

"Yeah," Rosie said, grinning.

Mrs. Wilder looked at her watch. "Oh, dear! Come, Claudia, let me show you around the house. Then I've *got* to go."

I felt numb as I followed her. Math, science, tap dance, ballet, voice, violin — was there *anything* this girl didn't do? Was there anything we'd even be able to talk about? I wouldn't know Mozart if I fell over him in the street.

Somehow, I didn't think I'd be needing the Kid-Kit I'd brought along.

Mrs. Wilder gave me all the usual instructions. Being a trained baby-sitter, I made sure to ask about emergency phone numbers, spare keys, and a bunch of other things.

Then she left in a hurry, waving good-bye and blowing kisses to her daughter. And there I was, alone with Rosie Wilder, the genius of Elm Street.

"Well," I said cheerfully, "I didn't mean to interrupt your practicing, so — "

"I practice till four-fifteen," Rosie said, looking at a clock on the living room mantel. "Then

I have a snack, and I then do my homework."

"Okay, great," I said. "I'll just hang out. If you need me, give a holler!"

Rosie stared at me. "Why would I need you?"

I shrugged. "I don't know. I meant, you know, if you — "

"Do you know the piece I was playing?"

"Piece?" It took me a minute to figure out what she meant. "Oh, the music! No, I don't. I don't play the piano."

"Then why would I need you?" Rosie asked again.

I took a deep breath. Keep smiling, Claudia, I said to myself. "You — you won't, I guess. I meant, I'll just go into the den and start my homework. Maybe we can, like, get to know each other when you have your snack."

That *really* excited Rosie. She turned her back, walked to the piano, and said, "Okay," so softly I could hardly hear her.

I retreated into the den and sat on the couch. I saw a TV, surrounded by bookshelves. I couldn't help noticing some of the book titles: *Preparing Your Preschooler for Success; Gifted Children: A Parents' Guide; That's My Kid! An Approach to Show-Biz Careers from One Month to Eighteen Years.*

Now I was getting the creeps. No *way* could I do my homework and not feel like a moron in a house like this. I reached into my bag and pulled out a box of Milk Duds. I popped one into my mouth, but as I put the box down on the coffee table, some of them spilled out.

I reached to pick them up, but suddenly I pulled my hand back. I stared at the coffee table. The composition was great — the open box, a lumpy pile of Milk Duds near the flap . . .

It was perfect for "Junk Food Fantasy." I pulled out my sketch pad and started drawing.

I became so involved in the project that I didn't notice when the piano playing stopped. I was sketching the edges of the table when I heard, "I thought you were doing homework."

"Huh?" I spun around to see Rosie staring over my shoulder. "Oh, I didn't hear you come in."

"Did you spill those?" Rosie asked.

"Uh, yes."

"And you're drawing them instead of picking them up?"

"Yeah," I said, closing up my pad. "I like to draw. I thought this would be . . . interesting."

Rosie gave me a blank look that I couldn't figure out. Then she scrunched up her brow and turned to leave. "I'm going to have my snack now."

"Okay, I'll be with you in a second," I said. I scooped up the Milk Duds and put them back in the box.

When I reached the kitchen, Rosie was taking a bowl of green grapes out of the refrigerator. "Want some?" she asked.

"Sure," I said.

We sat across from each other at the table, eating grapes. Rosie didn't say a word. "Would you like some Milk Duds?" I asked.

"I don't think they go with grapes," Rosie replied.

I tried to laugh, but it was hard. I hadn't even known Rosie an hour, and she was already getting on my nerves.

Getting on my nerves? I wanted to grab her by the collar and shake her.

But a good baby-sitter has patience, patience, patience. It's the secret to keeping your sanity — and your clients. "You sounded great," I said.

Rosie's face brightened a little. "I'm level four-plus in the district competition. Mrs. Wood says I'm double-A material." She looked at my blank expression, then added, "That's the highest grade," as if she were talking to the dumbest human being on Earth.

"Wow," I said, trying to look impressed. I spent the next few seconds trying to figure out something to say, then remembered her audition. "What are you auditioning for?"

"*Meet Me in St. Louis*," Rosie answered. "At the Hamlin Dinner Theater. It's for the role of Tootie — you know, the role Margaret O'Brien played in the movie. Do you want to see the song I'm preparing?"

"Okay," I said.

Before I could even finish the word, Rosie hopped out of her seat. "Come into the basement."

I followed her downstairs. The basement was set up like a dance studio — a *barre* along each wall, floor-to-ceiling mirrors, bright lights, and a cassette player on a table.

Rosie sat in a corner and changed into a pair of tap shoes. Then she stood up, flicked on the tape player, and ran to the center of the room. "Don't get too close," she said.

Some old-fashioned music started, and Rosie's face suddenly changed. It was as if someone had pasted a smile on her face. It was huge but fake.

The strangest thing was, there was something *familiar* about that smile. I couldn't figure out what.

Rosie began to sing a song I vaguely remember from an old Fred Astaire movie or something. Her voice was pretty good. Then she started tapping, and I was amazed. She *was* talented. I would have hired her in a minute if I were putting on that dinner-theater show.

Except for her smile. It bugged me.

After she finished I applauded. "That was fantastic!" I said.

Rosie turned off the tape. "Thanks. I can do ballet, too. Watch."

I sat down. She changed into ballet shoes and danced to a recording of *Swan Lake*.

Then I had to go upstairs and hear her play the violin.

I was expecting her to take out a tuba when she finally said, "Oh, well, I have to do my math homework now."

Intermission! I was thrilled. It's tough to look interested when someone half your age is showing off with things you could never do.

Rosie went into her room and I plopped myself on the couch in the den. I was going to start my own homework, but I heard Rosie call out, "Claudia?"

"Yes?" I answered, running down the hall to her room.

She was sitting at her desk, writing in a workbook. When I came in, she looked up and asked, "Do foxes hibernate?"

"Um . . . well, uh . . . I'm not sure," I said.

She squinted at me, as if she thought I was fooling her. "Didn't you take third-grade science?" she asked.

"Yes, but — "

"Did you pass it?"

"Yes!" I tried not to shout. "I just don't remember."

Rosie snorted a laugh through her nose. "I never forget the things I learn."

"Sorry," I said with a shrug. I wanted to kill her.

That afternoon was one of the longest in my life. I tried and tried to be nice and to get to know Rosie. We even went for a walk. I took the house keys and left a note for Mrs. Wilder — and Rosie corrected my spelling.

Corrected my *spelling!* Seven years old!

By the time Mrs. Wilder got back, I felt about three inches tall. I smiled. I said thank you. I said good-bye to Rosie.

But all the way home, I had only one thought.

Never again. Never in a million years.

CHAPTER 5

A million years took two days. On Thursday I went back to the Wilders' house as planned. And you know what? I felt good. At our Wednesday BSC meeting, I had told everyone about Rosie. Practical Kristy had made a great suggestion. She thought I should treat the job as a project. Each day I could try to set a few simple goals to make things go easier.

So Thursday was Day One of Operation Rosie. These were my simple goals:

1. To keep myself in a good mood, no matter what.

2. To finish two sketches while Rosie was practicing for her audition.

3. To call Janine if Rosie really needed help with her homework. (I had asked Janine about it, and she said it would be fine.)

Thursday was a perfect spring day, warm and breezy. I arrived at the Wilders' house just as a blue minivan pulled into the driveway. Mrs. Arnold, a BSC client, was driving Rosie home from school. Her twin daughters, Marilyn and Carolyn, were in the backseat with Buddy Barrett. Rosie was sitting in the front passenger seat.

"Hi, Claudia!" Mrs. Arnold called.

"Hi, Claudia!" Marilyn, Carolyn, and Buddy chimed in.

"Hi!" I yelled back, waving.

I guess Rosie figured there had been enough "Hi's" said already. She stepped out of the van and began walking silently toward the house.

As the van drove away, I said, "I got here just in time, huh?"

Rosie pulled a set of keys out of her backpack. "I'm early. I told Mrs. Arnold to drop me off first because I have so much to do."

"I know," I said. "With your audition practice and all . . ."

"Rehearsal," Rosie said, pushing the front door open.

"What?" I asked.

"It's called a *rehearsal*, not an audition practice. You *practice* for lessons. You *rehearse* for an audition or a performance."

I nodded politely and said to myself: Smile, Claudia, smile.

We walked inside, and Rosie plopped her backpack on the kitchen floor. In the center of the table was a note on yellow legal paper, which said:

Hi, Girls!
Claudia, there's some tuna salad in the fridge. Help yourself and put a scoop on a bed of lettuce for Rosie. There are fruit juices and soda, too. Just a reminder — Rosie has homework till 5:00, then preparation for her rehearsal, which begins at 5:15. Call me at 555-7660 if you need to.
Thanks. Love and kisses to Rosie!
Ginger

"Your mom says there's tuna salad," I said, heading for the refrigerator.

"I can read," Rosie replied.

I let that comment go. I kept my cool.

The tuna salad was in a covered glass bowl next to a container of washed lettuce. I found the plates and made two helpings. "Looks great," I said, putting the plates on the table.

"Actually I like chicken salad better," Rosie said, "but eating fish helps prevent blood cholesterol."

Cholesterol? She was worried about cholesterol at age seven? I didn't even know what the word meant at that age. I *still* don't!

We ate a few bites, and I was all set to ask Rosie about her school day, when she reached into her backpack and pulled out what looked like a big pamphlet. On the cover were a man and a woman in top hat and tails.

"What's that?" I asked.

Rosie rolled her eyes, giving me that I-can't-believe-she-doesn't-know look. "Sheet music," she said. She held it up to me.

"Oh," I said. "Is that your audition song?"

"Mm-hm." She pressed it open on the table. Then she took a bite of tuna salad and began humming. Soon her body was moving in rhythm, as if she were practicing.

I waited awhile, then said, "I thought you knew it just great the other day." With a big, complimentary smile, I added, "I can't even imagine why you'd need to practice — I mean, rehearse."

Rosie swallowed her tuna salad and said, "You don't know, Claudia. When you go to an audition, you're up against dozens of other kids with just as much talent as you. Not only do you have to be *perfect*, but you have to bring a special something to it. Something that sets you apart. And the only way you can do that is by rehearsing."

Rosie said that speech as if she had memorized it. She probably had, too. I was sure some agent or director had told her that. Maybe even Ginger Wilder.

"It's the same way with art," I said. Then I thought of a joke Stacey's father once told us in New York City. "Hey, Rosie, how do you get to Carnegie Hall?" I asked.

Rosie scrunched up her brow. "Well, you take the train to — "

"Practice!" I said.

"Huh?"

"Practice," I repeated. "That's how you get to Carnegie Hall. You practice." (For a moment I thought I might be using the wrong punch line. Was I supposed to say "rehearse"?)

Rosie gave me her famous stare. Then she put on this huge, fake smile and said, "Ha, ha, ha. Very funny."

And *that* was when I figured out why her smile looked familiar. In my mind I could see that same smile, but on a slightly younger girl, with one tooth missing. The girl had spilled a glass of chocolate milk, and her mom was going crazy over the stain on their rug.

"Rosie," I said, "were you in a TV commercial for a carpet cleaner?"

"Up 'n' Out Cleaner," Rosie said with a nod. "My dad says it's my college tuition."

I tried to figure that one out. "I don't get it."

"Residuals," Rosie whined. "You *know* . . . you get a check for every time the commercial airs, and it gets put in a *trust* fund. Then, when it's time to go to college, you have tons of money."

"Oh," I said.

Suddenly I wasn't hungry. *Rosie* was the girl on that dumb commercial! Not only did she have talent and brains, but she was rich . . . and famous. For spilling chocolate milk and smiling!

Rosie had already done more in her life than I probably *ever* would. She had even set aside money for college.

With a sigh, Rosie closed the music and got up. "I have to do science homework before my rehearsal." She took her plate to the sink. "Can you help me? It's a lot of work."

Maybe I could have helped her. But I didn't even want to try. The first words out of my mouth were, "I'll call my sister, Janine. She's a ge— she's really smart in science."

Rosie shrugged. "If you want. I think I'll do it on the front steps. It's stuffy in here."

As she walked toward the front door, I called home.

Fortunately Janine answered. "Kishi residence."

"Hi, Janine, it's me," I said.

"Hi, me," answered Janine. That's her idea of humor.

"Remember that favor we talked about yesterday?" I asked.

"Yup," Janine replied. "What's the address, 477 Elm?"

"Yeah."

"I'll be right over."

Thank goodness for Janine. Sometimes it really pays to have a brain for a sister.

I took my backpack and headed for the porch *slo-o-o-o-wly* (I hoped Janine would arrive soon and I wouldn't be stuck answering questions).

Rosie was sitting on the stoop, hunched over a textbook. She had put on a pair of tortoise-shell glasses that made her look even smarter than usual.

An old wicker chair was off to one side. I sat in it, pulled out my sketch pad, and began drawing.

Rosie didn't even look at me. Obviously she had given up thinking I knew *anything*.

Janine showed up around four-fifteen. I hopped out of the chair and said, "Rosie, this is my sister, Janine."

"I know," said Rosie. (I *knew* she'd say that.)

"Hi," Janine said shyly.

"Hi," replied Rosie. "You're good in science?"

"Pretty good," said Janine.

That was an understatement! "She's won all kinds of awards," I blurted out.

"Yeah?" said Rosie.

Janine sat down next to her. "Sort of. What do you need help in?"

For the next forty minutes or so, I felt as if I were in a foreign country. Finally I returned to my chair. I couldn't understand half of what was being said. Janine, in her glasses, was explaining things about animal migration and habitats. Rosie, in her glasses, was nodding and asking intelligent-sounding questions.

And Claudia Kishi, with no glasses, was drawing half a Twinkie. I felt about as useful as an oar on a speedboat.

You'd think even geniuses would get tired of talking about homework after awhile. Not those two. No joking around, no chatting, no fun at all.

A little before five o'clock, I heard Rosie say, "That's the last question."

I looked up from my Twinkie. Janine was still sitting up straight, with her hands folded in her lap. "Is there anything else I can help you with?" she asked.

"Uh-uh," said Rosie, shaking her head no. She closed her book, looked at her watch, and said, "I have to start getting ready for my rehearsal now."

Janine stood up stiffly. "Okay."

"You guys work everything out?" I asked cheerfully.

"Yeah," Rosie said. She turned to go inside, then called over her shoulder, "Thanks."

"You're welcome," said Janine. " 'Bye."

" 'Bye," answered Rosie as she disappeared inside.

I looked at Janine. She looked at me. "She's bright," said Janine.

"I know," I replied. "Thanks for helping me out."

Janine smiled. "It's okay. See you later."

"See you," I said as she walked away.

Oh, well, so they didn't become best buddies. At least I got a break from Rosie. And I think Janine really helped her.

When I went inside, Rosie was already clattering around in the basement with her tap shoes.

Pretty soon her teachers arrived. First came Mr. Bryan, her tap teacher. He was at least as old as my dad, but he had a body like a teenager's — not an ounce of fat. Then came Ms. Van Cott, the voice teacher. She had long blonde hair and a huge voice that echoed in the room when she spoke.

I was *thrilled* to let the two of them have full charge of Rosie for the next hour.

I went straight to the den with my sketch

pad. For awhile, though, I was distracted by the sounds downstairs. Ms. Van Cott began honking and bellowing, and Rosie would imitate her — some kind of voice exercises, I guess. Then the tape recording started. I could hear the click-clacking of tap dancing. Rosie's steps sounded something like this:

Tip-tip-ti-tap-tap-sssscrape-tip-tip!

Then Mr. Bryan would stop her, shouting, "Okay, okay, not quite! Give it more of a *lift*, like this . . ." *His* dancing sounded like *clackety-clack-click . . . stomp-stomp!*

It was pretty obnoxious. But after awhile I was able to tune it out. I returned to work on the Twinkie and managed to give it a kind of personality. I began feeling better. After twenty minutes or so I switched over to the Milk Duds drawing.

By that time the sounds from downstairs had grown awfully loud. Rosie was singing at the top of her lungs, not at all as nicely as she had sung the day before.

"Rosie dear, get it up into the *mask!*" Ms. Van Cott was shouting. "The soft palate! Lift the soft palate!"

"It's shuffle-shuffle-*falap*-step!" Mr. Bryan added.

"More head, less chest!" said Ms. Van Cott.

"You're getting behind on that double time step!" said Mr. Bryan.

Whoa. Poor Rosie! I never thought I'd feel sorry for her, but I did. The two teachers were getting carried away.

Fortunately (for Rosie), the lesson seemed to end soon afterward. I could tell because the music stopped and the teachers' voices grew quieter. Ms. Van Cott was telling Rosie to "warm down" (whatever *that* means), and Mr. Bryan kept saying, "And *stretch* . . . and *stretch!*" (Even with my small brainpower, I figured that meant he was leading her in stretching exercises.)

Before long the teachers bounced happily out of the house, calling good-bye to me.

I listened for Rosie, but I didn't hear her. For a moment I thought she might have collapsed with exhaustion.

Finally I heard her footsteps on the basement stairs. "Rosie?" I called. "How did it go?"

"Fine," she answered.

Her voice sounded hoarse, and that made me feel even worse for her. When she entered the den, she was drenched in sweat and her face was red.

"What a workout!" I said.

"Yeah," answered Rosie. Her eyes went from me to my sketch pad, which I had put on the coffee table. "Can I see?" she asked.

I was shocked. Rosie the Great, showing an

interest in *my* drawings? I held up my pad. "Sure."

Rosie stared at the Milk Duds for a long time without saying anything. Then she flipped to the Twinkie. "I hate these," she said.

"The drawings?" I asked.

"No, Twinkies." She flipped through some more drawings. "You erase a lot."

"Well, they're only sketches," I said. "I'm going to make paintings of them."

"Of *candy?*" she said with a little sneer.

I shrugged. "Why not? It's fun."

Rosie didn't answer. She kept flipping the pages, staring at each drawing.

"The Ring Ding is better than the others," she said.

"Thanks." It wasn't a rave review, but I had to take what I could get.

Rosie looked at all the sketches, then handed the pad back to me. "I like to draw sometimes," she said.

"Really?" I asked. I supposed she was going to say her art was appearing in a New York gallery.

"Yeah," she said. "A little. Well, I'm going to change and start working on a project before my mother comes home."

"You're done with homework?"

"Yup. When Janine was here."

"Okay." I decided to be daring. "Hey, if

you like to draw, how about working here with me?" I asked. I figured as long as we had *something* in common, there was hope.

Rosie turned around. I smiled. "It would be really relaxing," I said.

"That's okay," Rosie answered in a dull voice.

Then she turned and trudged up the stairs.

Oh, well. I had tried.

CHAPTER 6

Friday

Well, yesterday I became the first BSC member besides Claud to sit for Rosie. I had listened to everything you said, Claudia. I had made all kinds of plans. I thought I was well prepared.

I wasn't expecting the most embarrassing day of my whole baby-sitting career!

It started at Stoneybrook Elementary School. I had to go there to pick Rosie up, because her car pool had been canceled...

Thursday was the one day I couldn't sit for Rosie. And I have to admit, I was relieved.

Stacey got stuck with — oops, I mean Stacey got the job. I thought maybe it wouldn't be so bad for her. Maybe she and Rosie could get into a really exciting conversation about math (yawn).

I was wrong.

The job started well enough. Stacey wanted to make a good impression. She raced to SES after school so she wouldn't keep Rosie waiting. She arrived a moment after the final bell had rung. As the kids streamed outside, Stacey took a good long look at the photo of Rosie I'd given her (I had asked Mrs. Wilder to give me a copy of Rosie's professional photo, because Stacey had never met Rosie).

It wasn't hard to spot that thick red hair. Rosie was with a group of four other girls, all chatting away.

Stacey could hear every word. They were talking about Disney World. "I wasn't even afraid of Space Mountain," one of them said.

"Neither was I," said another. "It was fun."

"I know," said a third one. "*I've* been there five times. My grandparents live near there."

"I've been there three times," piped up a fourth girl.

"I had a picture taken with Mickey Mouse,"

said the second girl. "He was really an actor, and I could see his eyes through the costume."

Finally Rosie spoke up. "*I* had to wear a costume like that, too."

"At Disney World?" the second girl said. "They let kids work there?"

"No," Rosie answered loudly. "In a *commercial*. It's for cat food, and it's airing next month. I wear this kitten costume, and I feed some food to a real cat, then I take off my mask and the cat runs away — "

"What's that got to do with Disney World?" asked the third girl.

"I bet you've never even been there, Rosie," said the fourth one with a sneer.

Rosie grew red in the face. "Well — it's only because *I* have a *career!* I'm too busy to do baby stuff like go to Disney World — "

"Cut it out, Rosie," the first girl said. "You're just jealous."

That was where Stacey stepped in. "Hi . . . are you Rosie?"

"Yeah," said Rosie, still scowling.

"I'm Stacey. I'm going to walk you home."

Rosie answered with her two favorite words. "I know."

The girls said good-bye. Two of them were headed in the same direction as Rosie and Stacey, but they made sure to cross to the other side of the street.

Stacey felt bad for Rosie, but she knew how the other girls must have felt. Rosie was *not* easy to like.

"So, I hear you're a really good singer and tap dancer," Stacey said.

"Yeah," said Rosie.

"And good in math and science," Stacey went on.

Rosie nodded. "English, too. I'm in the Grand Crossword Competition next week."

"Really?" said Stacey.

"Do you know what it is?" asked Rosie.

"Uh . . . no," Stacey admitted. "I guess it's a crossword puzzle contest, right?"

"The school *finals*," Rosie corrected her. "First I won the competition in my class, and then in the whole third grade. Now I go up against the fourth- and fifth-graders. It's going to be in the auditorium next Thursday. They put three huge puzzles on blackboards on stage, and we each work on one. The first person to complete one correctly wins."

"Sounds like fun," Stacey said. "Maybe I can help you prepare this afternoon."

"No," Rosie said. "Uncle Dandy's coming over. Didn't my mom tell you?"

"Uncle *who?*" asked Stacey.

"Uncle Dandy!" Rosie said. "You don't know about him?"

"No."

Rosie exhaled impatiently. "It was in all the papers. He's going to be the host of a talent show on TV called *Uncle Dandy's Star Machine*. It's going to be on Channel 3, with kids from all over central Connecticut."

"Wow," said Stacey. "Did he see you in a show or something?"

"No, my agent contacted him. She's bringing him over at four-thirty."

"Four-thirty?" said Stacey. "Aren't you nervous? Do you know what you're going to perform?"

"I'm never nervous," answered Rosie. "First I'm going to do my new tap number, then play the piano and the violin, then do a scene from a soap opera. See, we're not sure which of my talents Uncle Dandy will want to use on the show."

"So you'll do a little of everything," said Stacey.

"Right."

Sure enough, when Stacey reached Rosie's house, she found a note from Mrs. Wilder on the kitchen table. It told about Uncle Dandy's visit, and politely suggested that Stacey do her homework in the den during the audition. (In other words, make herself scarce.)

Rosie didn't agree. "You can watch if you want," she said. "I don't mind."

Stacey compromised. She set up her

schoolwork in the Wilders' dining room. From there she could see part of the living room, where Rosie was going to do the music and acting parts of her audition. The dance part was going to take place in the basement.

Rosie went downstairs to practice her tap number. Stacey began studying. Then, at four twenty-five, *Stacey's* stomach went into knots. She didn't know why. Can you imagine? So-phisticated Stacey, who used to see famous people on the sidewalks of New York every day, nervous about meeting Uncle Dandy!

Actually I think she was nervous for Rosie. Stacey felt a lot more sympathetic to her than I did. She says conceited people are actually insecure.

I didn't believe it. *Insecure* was about the last word I'd use to describe Rosie.

Well, it wasn't until a quarter to five that the doorbell rang. "Can you get that?" Rosie called from the basement. "I'm practicing my pullbacks."

(Huh?)

"Sure," answered Stacey.

She went to the door, opened it, and saw a glamorous-looking Asian-American woman wearing a silk scarf and a long, flowing dress. Next to her was a heavyset (all right, *fat*) man with a bright smile and thick blond hair. Stacey didn't want to stare, but she was sure he was wearing a toupee.

"Hi, I'm Dan Beasley, otherwise known as Uncle Dandy," the man said. "Are you Mary Rose?"

"No, she's the baby-sitter, Dan," the woman said as Stacey opened the door. "Hello, dear, I'm Rosie's agent, Sandra Yu. I'm so sorry we're late."

"That's okay," Stacey said. "Rosie's in the basement. She's practicing her backpulls."

"Sounds dangerous," Uncle Dandy said with a laugh.

Stacey cringed. She knew she had gotten the word wrong. She slunk back to her homework as the other two walked downstairs.

Rosie performed her tap number, and Stacey said it sounded great. Uncle Dandy clapped loudly and yelled, "Brava!" (Janine explained that you say that to a girl, instead of "Bravo!")

Soon Rosie, Sandra Yu, and Uncle Dandy trooped upstairs and Rosie played some complicated "piece" on the piano. Uncle Dandy clapped loudly at that, too, and at Rosie's violin playing (despite a couple of embarrassing squeaks).

Then came Rosie's acting. Stacey could see Rosie clearly as she stepped into the middle of the living room with a script in her hands.

"I shall perform a selection from the daytime

television serial *The Brash and the Beautiful*," Rosie announced in a singsong voice. "It's the part of Josephine, the runaway girl. In this scene, she meets her father after having escaped from a home for wayward children, where she was treated terribly and lost her memory. For this scene, I shall require someone to read the part of the father."

"Sweetheart, can't you do a monolog instead?" Ms. Yu asked her.

Rosie frowned. "I don't have one *prepared*," she replied. "Besides, you said I was perfect for this role — "

"Yes, yes, of course," Ms. Yu answered. "Uh, Dan, what's your policy on scene auditions?"

"*I* could read the part," Uncle Dandy said, "but not without my glasses. I'm liable to hold the thing upside down and sound like I'm reading Russian — har har!"

"I know!" Rosie said. Then she called out, "Stacey?"

Stacey gulped. She thought she was hearing things. Rosie couldn't *possibly* expect her to —

"Stacey, will you read with me?" Rosie called.

The house fell silent. Rosie, Uncle Dandy, and Ms. Yu stared at Stacey. Her heart started beating like crazy. "Uh . . . okay."

Stacey was stuck. How could she say no?

She walked into the room, feeling as if she were going to pass out. She stood next to Rosie and looked at the script. "Start here," Rosie whispered, pointing to a place that said SCENE 3.

Stacey cleared her throat. " 'Dad answers knock,' " she read.

"No, that's a stage direction!" Rosie said.

"Oh, sorry. Uh . . . 'Who could be bothering me at this hour? Yes, what can I — ' "

" 'You got anything to drink?' " Rosie said in a dull, flat voice.

It said *pause*, so Stacey paused. " 'Darling,' " she said. Then it said, *He stares at her*, so Stacey stared at Rosie, then lost her place. "Uh . . . wait a minute . . . oh! Here! Um, 'It can't be. Oh, darling, my darling, it's you!' "

" 'Leave me alone, you creep, I'm thirsty,' " Rosie said.

" 'But my sweet, dear Josy, my love. Don't you remember? It's me, Daddy!' " Then it said, *He grabs her by the shoulders and kisses her*, but Stacey decided against that. " 'Daddy, who changed your diapers. Daddy, who sang, "Hush little baby, don't say a word, Poppa's gonna buy you a mockingbird . . ." ' "

Stacey was *dying*. This was so embarrassing!

(I would have given *anything* to have been there.)

Anyway, Rosie dropped her script on the

floor. She turned to Stacey and gawked with her mouth hanging open. " 'D-D-Daddy?' " she whispered.

Stacey tried to look at the script on the floor. She bent down, thinking she must have had a line.

Then Rosie threw her arms around Stacey, practically tackling her. " 'Daddy!' " she shrieked. " 'Oh, Daddy! Oh, I love you so! I love you! Am I home? Am I really, really home?' "

"Um . . ." Stacey wrestled out of Rosie's grip. But when she bent to pick up the script, she stepped on it. She heard a huge *rrrrrip* as it tore in half. Stacey picked up the pieces and frantically looked for her line.

Rosie stood by the piano, ad-libbing "Oh, Daddys" and crying dramatically.

"Uh . . ." Stacey said. "Uh . . ."

Ms. Yu finally spoke up. "I think that covers the dramatic ground nicely," she said. "Don't you, Dan?"

"Yes, very nice," Uncle Dandy said, smiling at Rosie. "Very emotional. Thank you so much for sharing your talent, Mary Rose. You'll be on my show, all right. When I figure out in what capacity, I'll call Ms. Yu right away."

He stood up, shook Rosie's hand, and left with Ms. Yu. Neither of them even *looked* at Stacey.

When Stacey turned around, she saw Rosie's eyes filled with tears. Stacey wasn't sure if she was acting or if they were for real.

Rosie went straight to a tissue box and blew her nose. Then she said calmly, as if nothing had happened, "I've got something to do in my room. Call me when my mother comes."

Stacey didn't have the strength to answer. She felt about two inches tall.

CHAPTER 7

Five-eighteen.

I looked at the clock out of the corner of my eye. It was Monday evening, four days after Stacey's fateful evening with Rosie. I was hard at work on my painting, *Milk Duds, Spilled*.

Yes, painting. Over the weekend I'd started turning my sketches into the real thing. On Sunday I finished *Twinkie Unwrapped*, and it had turned out really well. The colors were rich, and made you hungry just looking at the painting.

Milk Duds was harder to do. At the moment, the Duds resembled metal balls, and I was determined to fix them.

At five-twenty, I realized I needed a lot more time. I'd have to wait till after the meeting to finish. Meanwhile, my room was a war zone, and I had to clean up in a hurry.

I shoved my paints and brushes into the closet. Then I scooped up the old newspapers

I'd laid out to protect the floor and ran downstairs to put them in the recycling pile. My canvases weren't so easy to put away, though. I just leaned them against the walls of my room.

When Kristy showed up, her eyes zeroed in on the two canvases. She laughed.

"What's so funny?" I asked.

"I don't know," Kristy said. "Those just . . . make me laugh."

"Thanks a *lot*," I said.

"No, no! I'm not laughing *at* them. They make me feel good. It's a compliment, Claud. I think they're great."

I was excited to hear Kristy say that. Especially after her first reaction to my project, back in the beginning.

Soon the others showed up, and Kristy called the meeting to order. I passed around the usual junk food.

"Any new business?" Kristy asked.

"I have some," I said. "On Friday, Mrs. Wilder told me she's going to need us for at least another week. Her mom's still not better."

Kristy nodded. "Mary Anne?" she said.

Mary Anne checked her book. "Claudia, you're free Tuesday and Friday. You've got Charlotte Johanssen on Thursday, but Kristy's free that day, and so's Stacey and Jessi — "

"Uh, count me out," Stacey said. Then she smiled and added, "Please. I'm still recovering from the last time."

"I don't want to be part of any audition," Kristy said. "I'd die."

There was an embarrassed silence. Fortunately Mary Anne saved the day. "Look, we're talking about Rosie like she's a monster. She's human, too, you know."

"I know," I said, "but she's so . . . pushy. She's got all this talent, but she uses it like a machine."

"She *is* like a machine," said Stacey. "I mean, *you* work hard on your art, Claudia, but you love it. It shows. Rosie always looks so . . . *grim*. Or else she has this forced smile. I don't think she really likes what she's doing."

"Yeah," I said. "She's not a very happy girl."

"Maybe her parents are pushing her," Mary Anne suggested. "Maybe we should encourage her to loosen up, have more fun."

"Maybe we should take her to a fun *kids'* place, like the zoo," suggested Mal.

"It would probably interfere with some lesson," I said.

Then Jessi spoke up. "*I'd* like to take that Thursday job with Rosie. She's into dance, right? We have that in common. Maybe we'll get along."

"That might work," Mary Anne said.

"Uh-oh," Dawn exclaimed suddenly. She was looking at Kristy, who was obviously thinking hard. "Kristy's working on an idea — "

"Boy, do I have a great idea!" Kristy blurted out.

Dawn giggled. "I thought so."

"What?" said Mal and Stacey and I at the same time.

Kristy glanced at me. "You should have a show!"

"Huh?" I said. "What does that have to do with Rosie?"

"It doesn't," Kristy said. "But I was looking at your paintings, and it just popped into my head. You should have an art show, Claudia. I mean, why should your paintings sit up here where nobody can enjoy them?"

"*We'll* enjoy them," I replied.

"I know, but the *public* should see them, Claud," Kristy insisted.

"Yeah, but where? I can't just walk into a gallery and ask someone to give me an exhibit!"

"Make your own gallery," Kristy said. "Your garage! We could have an opening and invite all our kids. They would love it, and the subject of junk food is perfect. It would show them that art can be fun."

I hadn't thought of being so public with my paintings, but a show *did* sound like fun. And if I was going to be a famous artist someday, this would be good practice. "I guess we *could*," I said. "I'd need some help cleaning the garage, though. It's a pigsty."

"With seven of us, it'll take no time," Kristy said. Everyone nodded enthusiastically.

"I could easily hang the paintings on the wall," I said, "and the lighting's not bad. I guess I'd have to figure out a date I could be finished; then that'll be the opening."

"It'll also give you something definite to shoot for," Stacey said. "I bet you'll work twice as fast."

"Yup," I said. "Then we can send invitations to my neighbors and all our clients — "

"And serve junk food as refreshments!" Kristy chimed in. "It's perfect!"

Well, I was pretty excited by then. We all were. Soon phone calls began interrupting us, but in between them we kept planning and talking.

Everyone was in a great mood when Kristy adjourned the meeting at six o'clock. I was thrilled. *My first show!* But boy, did I have a lot of work to do. I pulled out my *Milk Duds* canvas for a quick touch-up before dinner.

My brush was in hand when the phone rang. (One of the only bad things about my bedroom being BSC headquarters is that parents sometimes call during nonmeeting hours.)

"Hello, Baby-sitters Club," I said impatiently.

"May I have Claudia, please?" It was Rosie's voice.

"Hi, Rosie, it's me," I said. "What's up?"

"You won't need to come tomorrow," she answered. "My agent just called to tell me I have a commercial booking in the city tomorrow. My mom's going to take me in while my aunt takes care of Grandma."

"Congratulations, Rosie!" I said. "What's the commercial for?"

"The phone company," she said. "I play a girl calling her grandfather in Norway or something."

"Great!" I said. "I can't wait to see it."

"I'll get a tape of it, I guess," she said. "See you Thursday."

"Uh . . . no, *Friday*," I said. "A different sitter is coming on Thursday — Jessi Ramsey. She's a great dancer. You'll love her."

"Oh," Rosie said in a soft voice. "Well, 'bye."

" 'Bye," I said. "And good luck!"

"You mean, 'Break a leg.' "

"What?"

"You're supposed to say, 'Break a leg' to

70

actors. It's good luck to wish bad luck and vice versa."

That was Rosie — even correcting a compliment. "Well, break *two* legs!" I said cheerfully.

"Thanks," said Rosie, " 'Bye."

" 'Bye."

I hung up the phone, feeling really excited for Rosie.

And, to tell the truth, I was relieved that I'd miss *two* days with her that week.

CHAPTER 8

Thursday

Today was my turn to sit for Rosie Wilder. I felt excited, believe it or not. I even brought my toe shoes. When I was Rosie's age, I thought dancing _en pointe_ was like magic. I guess I thought she'd think so, too.

Okay, so things didn't turn out the way I expected. At least I tried. Too bad I'll probably never get the chance to try again...

Jessi was being hard on herself. She really did do a good job. But Rosie was being . . . Rosie. Here's what happened.

Jessi got to the Wilders' a little early. She waited for Rosie's car pool, which turned out to be a station wagon driven by Mrs. Barrett.

There were lots of "Hi, Jessi's" and waves from everyone in the car, but only a grunt from Rosie. The same treatment Stacey and I had gotten.

But Jessi knew enough to expect it. She wasn't even fazed. "Aren't you going to say hello?" she asked.

Rosie walked past her and opened the front door. "I did."

"Oh, I guess I didn't hear you," Jessi said as they both walked inside. "Hey, how did your commercial go?"

"How do you know about that?" asked Rosie.

"Claudia told us. My friends and I were all excited. It must be so much fun to be on TV."

Rosie shrugged. "I guess. You know, *five* of my commercials have already been on the air." She went into the kitchen and put her backpack on the floor. "I have them on tape."

"Yeah? Can we watch them?" Jessi was being very smart. She figured flattery was the way to get on Rosie's good side.

"Well, I have to do homework for forty-five minutes before my voice lesson," Rosie said, looking at the clock. "But if we eat our snack really fast, we'll have enough time."

Mrs. Wilder had left her usual note, explaining Rosie's schedule and asking the girls to help themselves to peanut butter-and-jelly sandwiches.

Jessi and Rosie made the sandwiches quickly and wolfed them down. Then they ran into the den. Jessi settled on the couch as Rosie put a videotape in the VCR.

"The first one is the best," she said, standing by the TV.

It was the carpet cleaner commercial. "I've seen this!" Jessi said. "That was you?"

"*Sssh!*" said Rosie. On the screen, the carpet gremlins were racing across the carpet, eating cartoon dirt with their cartoon teeth. "This was the hardest part. I was only *pretending* to see the creatures. They're animated, and they were added later. That expression on my face was just acting. Watch . . ."

Rosie rewound it and played it again — in *slow motion!* She made sure to tell Jessi every last detail of her acting "technique."

Jessi nodded politely and kept nodding through the rest of the commercials. When the tape was over, she said, "You were great!"

"Thanks," Rosie said. "I took a kids' commercial class in New York City. It gave me great practice and exposure."

"Uh-huh." Jessi wanted to talk about dancing. So she said, "Did you study ballet in New York, too?"

"A little bit, with a guy who used to dance with American Ballet Theater."

Jessi was impressed. "Wow! Who — "

"What grade are you in?" Rosie interrupted.

"Sixth," Jessi answered.

"Are you good at vocabulary?"

"Uh, well . . ." Vocabulary? What did that have to do with ballet class? Jessi was wondering. "Pretty good, I guess. Why?"

"I have to do some practice puzzles for the Crossword Competition," Rosie said, picking up her backpack. "Come help me."

Jessi followed Rosie upstairs. She was frustrated that the conversation about dance had stopped. If Rosie liked dance so much, why didn't she want to talk about it? Was she afraid Jessi might try to show her up?

Rosie's room was painted a light salmon color with white moldings. Next to her blond-wood desk was a floor-to-ceiling shelf stuffed with books. The wall was full of photos: Rosie with TV stars, Rosie on the set of a commercial, Rosie singing at a recital, Rosie in a local production of *Fiddler on the Roof*, Rosie playing the violin in an orchestra. You get the idea.

Rosie pulled a large book out of her pack and set it on her desk. Its title was *Crossword Fun — from Beginner to Advanced*. She opened it to a puzzle that was half-filled with letters.

"This is a hard one," she said, sitting down. "Let's see . . . Fifteen Down: 'A three-toed sloth.' Two letters. What's that?"

"Uh . . . I don't know," Jessi said. "How about one of the Across words that shares a square with it?"

"Fifteen Across," Rosie replied. " 'Ansel *Blank*, American photographer.' Five letters."

Jessi shook her head. "Let's try another."

"I thought you said you had a good vocabulary," Rosie remarked. "How about Twenty-three Across. 'Jurassic giant.' Eleven letters beginning with A, P."

Huh?

By then Jessi's alarm signal was going off. She felt completely useless, but an emergency plan popped into her head. "You know Janine Kishi, right?" she said. "She's *much* better at this than I am. I'll call her."

"Wait — " Rosie started to protest. But Jessi ran to the downstairs phone and called our house.

Janine answered right away. "Kishi residence."

"Hi, Janine, it's Jessi Ramsey."

"Hi, Jessi. Claudia's at the Johanssens'. Do you have their number?"

"Yeah, but I wanted to talk to *you*. Um, Claudia told me you once helped Rosie Wilder with her homework . . ."

"I made what I considered a valiant attempt," Janine said.

"Well, I'm sitting for her right now, and . . . I know you must be really busy, but I was wondering if you could come over for a few minutes. She needs help doing crossword puzzles. It's for a school contest."

Janine laughed. "I guess I'm becoming Rosie's official tutor."

"I'm sorry, Janine," Jessi said quickly. "I didn't mean to — "

"No, no, it's okay," Janine said. "I can take a break. I'll be right over."

"Thanks!"

"You're welcome. 'Bye."

When Jessi went back upstairs, Rosie didn't even look up from her book. "Janine's on her way," Jessi said.

"Uh-huh," mumbled Rosie.

"Do you want me to try helping you on some other clues?" asked Jessi.

"Nope."

"Okay, then I'll go downstairs and do some homework. Call me if you need me."

"Uh-huh."

Jessi had barely settled herself on the couch in the den when Janine rang the doorbell. "Boy, am I glad to see you," Jessi said.

"You ought to make me an honorary member of the Baby-sitters Club," Janine replied with a smile. "Where's Rosie?"

"At the top of the stairs," said Jessi. "In her room."

Janine went up to Rosie's room. Jessi returned to the den and breathed a sigh of relief.

But not for long. The walls in the Wilder house must be pretty thin, because Jessi could hear just about every word spoken upstairs.

Janine began the conversation with a friendly "Hi."

Rosie's reply was, "What's a two-letter word for a three-toed sloth?"

Janine paused a moment, then said, "Ai. A,I."

Jessi nearly dropped her notebook. She couldn't believe Janine actually *knew* that.

"A,I?" Rosie replied. "Are you sure?"

"Pretty sure."

"How did you know?"

"It's a word people use a lot in Scrabble," Janine answered. (I have to admit, I should have known it, too, because I'm the one Janine beats in Scrabble with words like *ai*!)

Janine also knew that a Jurassic giant was

an *apatosaurus*, and the photographer was Ansel *Adams*, and a bunch of other hard answers.

Well, you'd think Rosie would be happy to get such expert help, right?

Wrong.

Rosie kept giving Janine clues, pausing sometimes to answer them herself. Whenever Janine didn't know the answer, Rosie would exhale loudly as if Janine were really stupid. At one point Rosie remarked, "You're in *high school?*" because Janine didn't know a three-letter word for "Southwest Asian musical instrument of the lute family."

"Yes, I am," Janine snapped. She must have been really upset, because Janine *never* acts that way.

The next thing Jessi knew, Janine was poking her head in the den. "See you, Jessi," she said.

"Is everything all right?" Jessi asked.

"Mm-hm. Rosie doesn't need me anymore, that's all. 'Bye."

" 'Bye."

As Janine walked to the front door, Rosie came downstairs and headed for the refrigerator. She pulled out a carton of orange juice and poured herself a glass.

"Time to get ready for your voice lesson?" Jessi asked.

Rosie gulped down the juice, set her glass on the kitchen table, and said, "From now on, I only want Claudia to sit for me!"

That took Jessi by surprise. "Okay," she said calmly. "I'll bring it up at our next meeting. Maybe we can work it out."

"Good."

"Can I ask why?"

That's when Jessi noticed the tears in Rosie's eyes. "Because I like her the best!" she cried out.

Then she stomped up the stairs and into her room and slammed the door behind her.

CHAPTER 9

"Yuck. These markers come off on your hands!" Dawn said.

Kristy ran her index finger along a piece of paper that said PRIVATE INVI TION in red marker. (The "TA" in INVITATION had already been wiped off.) "It isn't the markers," she announced. "It's the glossy paper. We should return it to the store and get the regular kind."

"You mean like oak tag?" Stacey asked. "That's so dull-looking. These invitations have to look chic!"

"There's nothing chic about a piece of shiny paper full of smudges," Kristy said.

Jessi lifted up the paper and turned it around. "Hey, the back has a dull finish."

"I still think it would make more sense just to write up something simple and make photocopies of it," Mary Anne suggested.

"Not after we bought all these markers," Stacey said.

"Besides, this is a special event!" exclaimed Mal.

It was Saturday, a nonmeeting day, but the entire BSC had gathered in my room. As you probably guessed, we were going to send out invitations to the "Junk Food Fantasy" opening at the Claudia Kishi Gallery.

Well, maybe I shouldn't say *we*. Since I was the featured artist, I got to paint. The others had to worry about the invitations.

I was deeply involved in a new Gummi series. I'd finished *Gummi Bears* and was now working on *Gummi Worms*. I was concentrating really hard, so I only picked up pieces of the conversation around me.

"Let's make a rough draft," Mal said, taking out a piece of looseleaf paper. "Okay, what information do we want on the invitation?"

"The date and time, the name of the exhibit, the name of the gallery," Kristy said.

Mal began to write.

"We can say, 'Come one, come all — ' " Kristy began.

Stacey interrupted her. "No, that sounds like the circus. For an art exhibit you have to say something more sophisticated."

"Something sophisticated about *junk food?*"

Dawn said. "It should be fun, like the paintings."

"Okay, what?" Kristy asked.

Silence.

"Maybe we should put a miniature version of one of the paintings on each invitation," Jessi said.

"Oh, no!" I piped up. "I have enough work to do."

"Oooh, I know!" Dawn blurted out. "We could take actual candy wrappers and, like, glue them to the invitations."

Kristy shook her head. "Not practical. They'd get crushed in the mail, and it would look like we put trash in the envelopes by mistake. And what if there were still little bits of chocolate inside the wrappers — "

"Let's just say something simple," Mary Anne suggested. " 'You are invited to the opening of *Junk Food Fantasy*, a series of paintings by Claudia Kishi, in the Kishi garage,' and so on."

"Did you write that down, Mal?" Jessi asked.

"Wait," Mal said, scribbling furiously. " ' . . . a series of . . .' what?"

Well, now you know the secret of the Baby-sitters Club. We may be excellent baby-sitters, but that doesn't mean we're good at everything. Like making invitations.

After about an hour, my friends had finally sketched a decent-looking invitation. It didn't include any cute pictures of junk food, or even a title (we thought it would be fun to surprise people with the subject when they arrived) — just a simple message in elegant handwriting. We decided to make copies on card stock (thick paper).

Then we had to decide who to send them to.

First we were going to send them only to regular clients, but that seemed too selective. Then we were going to post an invitation in the local supermarket, but we thought too many strangers would come.

Finally we made up a list of about forty names of friends, clients, relatives.

That left even more questions. Who was going to go to the copy shop? Who was going to buy the stamps and envelopes? Who was going to address the invitations?

A half hour later, everyone was tired and cranky. I had set aside *Gummi Worms* to take part in the discussion (okay, *argument*). Finally Kristy brought up something we'd been putting off. "Claud, how long will it take to clean your garage?"

I pictured it in my mind: the mounds of old newspapers, the old tools that had been thrown into corners, the spare tires Dad hadn't thrown out . . .

"Uh, if we start today," I said, scratching my chin, "about five or six years."

It was supposed to be a joke, but hardly anyone even smiled. "I have to leave in an hour," Jessi said.

"I have to be home by three o'clock," Stacey said.

Kristy stood up. "I guess we'd better get started."

We went outside. Sure enough, the garage was a *major* disaster area. We started our work by bundling up the newspapers, and I promised to ask my parents to take the piles to the recycling center. Then we collected the useless-looking stuff, like a snow shovel with a broken handle and all those tires. We put them against the wall so I could ask Dad about them.

Needless to say, this was not one of the most fun Saturday afternoons in BSC history. And soon the complaints started.

One of the tires left a black mark on Stacey's new jeans. "Ucchh," she said. "I just washed these."

"I don't know where you intend to put all the stuff that's hanging on the hooks," Dawn said.

"I think the lighting is too dim," Mal remarked.

Mary Anne let out a sigh. "It looks so . . . grungy in here."

"It'll be fine," Kristy said impatiently. "Let's just get it done so we can enjoy at least *part* of the day."

That did it. This project was important to me, and everyone was acting as if we were in prison. I had to say something. "You know, if you don't like doing this, then why are you doing it?"

I must have seemed angry, because everyone gave me a concerned look. "We *have* to, Claud," said Mary Anne. "You need us to."

"But everyone's in such a bad mood," I said. "All I hear is complaining. If it's not going to be fun — "

"Oh, Claud, don't take it personally," said Mary Anne gently.

"Every fun project begins with some dirty work," Stacey added. "But you do it because it has to get done. There's no law that says you have to *like* every single thing you do, right?"

Everyone nodded.

"I guess," I mumbled.

Stacey's words were tumbling around in my head. They made a lot of sense, but for some reason, I was thinking of Rosie.

I pictured her sitting glumly over her crossword books, plastering a smile on her face while she tap-danced, reciting her list of achievements.

There's no law that says you have to like everything you do, Stacey had said.

What an interesting choice of words.

Maybe Rosie did her activities because she felt she *had* to. And just maybe none of us knew Rosie — *really* knew her — at all.

CHAPTER 10

"What's 'A Tennessee Williams classic: *A Streetcar Named* Blank,' a six-letter word ending with E?"

It was the third question Rosie had asked me. And it was the third question that made absolutely no sense to me.

Rosie had decided to study in the kitchen that evening, which was a Tuesday. At first I was very patient. Jessi had told me what Rosie had said about me, so I figured this was Rosie's way of getting closer.

But the minute I arrived at the Wilders', Rosie began tormenting me.

"Charlie?" I suggested.

Rosie shook her head. "That's seven letters."

"I don't know . . . how about Bobby?" I tried.

Rosie rolled her eyes. *"That* doesn't end in

E. Okay, how about this one . . . 'A four-sided figure with only two sides parallel'? Nine letters, the first two are T, R, and the seventh is O."

"Let me see," I said. I looked closely at the puzzle (as if that would help). After a moment I said, "I'm not that great in geometry."

"*Trapezoid!*" Rosie announced. "That's what it is!" She began scribbling madly.

"Rosie, if you already knew the answer, why did you ask me?"

"I *didn't* know it right away," she insisted. "It just came to me!"

I let out a sigh. My plan had been to work on a full-color sketch at the kitchen table. Now it looked like the kitchen was going to be a torture chamber the rest of the evening.

"Ten Across, 'A bi-valve mollusk,' seven letters, the second letter is Y," Rosie said.

I just shrugged.

"Hmmm, Ten Down is 'A Norse god,' four letters, ending in I, N," Rosie barged on. "I know that! *Odin*, and that makes the other word begin with O, Y . . . it's a mollusk . . . I think that's like a clam . . . oooh! *Oyster!* That's got to be it!"

"Great, Rosie," I said.

"Now, how about Twenty Across, 'A — ' "

That was all I could take. "The opposite of

yes," I said. "Two letters, beginning with N!"

"Huh?"

"N, O. No," I said. "I'm not going to answer any more questions. I never get them right, and I don't know why you keep asking me. Besides, you're much better at this than I am, and I have things of my own to do!"

Whew. That was the first time I'd ever talked to Rosie like that. For all I knew, it was the first time *anyone* ever did.

But you know what? I didn't care. For three weeks my friends and I had been bending over backward to please her. And all she did was antagonize us. It was time *someone* stood up to the great Rosie Wilder.

I expected Rosie either to stomp out of the kitchen furiously or cry. She did neither. She just nodded meekly and looked back at her book.

Then I felt guilty. For a minute I thought about apologizing to her.

But only for a minute.

Instead I reached into my backpack, which was beside my chair. I pulled out a couple of sketch pads, some pencils, and a bag of junk food.

I was working on four different sketches — a lollipop, a marshmallow, a bag of Doritos, and a Mounds bar. I opened one of my pads and turned to the lollipop sketch.

This one was going to burst with colors. With big, circular strokes, I drew broad swirls in the lollipop.

"A Streetcar Named Detour . . . Design . . . Derail . . ." Rosie muttered. Pages shuffled loudly as she leafed through her dictionary every few seconds.

The lollipop finally looked right. I tried out color combinations with my pencils. The background would be white, to make the colors really stand out.

Soon I had completely tuned Rosie out. I moved on to the Doritos sketch. First I had to get the model just right. I crunched and bunched the bag to give it the right angles. I discovered I could make it into a shape that was almost human. *That's* what I would draw.

As I was sketching, I noticed that Rosie had stopped working. Not only that, she was staring at me.

I figured she was stuck on a ten-letter word for some obscure European writer or something. And I wasn't going to give her the opportunity to ask me, so I pretended not to see her.

Next thing I knew, she was reaching across

the table. She took one of my sketch pads and ripped a page off the top.

She's testing me, I thought. Taking one of *my* pieces of paper just to get a rise out of me. I kept on working.

Not until about ten minutes later did I notice that Rosie was acting a little unusual. She would pause, look straight ahead, scribble something. Pause, look, scribble. Pause, look, scribble.

Then I saw her adjust the Mounds bar.

Finally I glanced at her. To my surprise, I realized she wasn't working on her puzzle at all.

She was drawing.

An outline of a Mounds bar was on her paper. Her lines were delicate and very accurate. The letters of the word MOUNDS were wrinkled along with the wrinkles in the wrapper.

My jaw practically dropped open. Rosie was *good!*

I shouldn't have been surprised. Rosie was talented at everything else. Why shouldn't she be good at drawing?

But I'll tell you what really interested me. Her face was relaxed, concentrated, and happy. She wasn't grim and scowling, the way she looked when she played the piano or the violin, or super smily, the way she looked when she tap-danced. She actually seemed to be enjoying herself.

"That's great, Rosie," I said. "You have a real flair for this!"

"Thanks," Rosie replied with a shy smile. "This is what I *really* like to do."

I couldn't believe it. Rosie looked like a modest little . . . seven-year-old girl!

Suddenly I understood why she only wanted me to baby-sit for her. She wanted to watch me draw. But why didn't she ever say so? Why did she always run up to her room and —

"Rosie," I said, "all those times you've gone up to your room to work on a project . . . have you really been practicing your drawing?"

Rosie's eyes lit up. But before she could say a word, the front door slammed.

"I'm home!" called a deep, cheerful male voice.

I rose from the table and began to answer, but Rosie waved her hand and said, *"Ssshhhh!"*

I turned back around. Rosie was shoving her Mounds drawing across the table, burying it under my pile. Her eyes were wide with panic.

Frantically she opened her crossword book and her dictionary. She grabbed a pencil, hunched herself over the book, and called out softly, "Hi, Daddy."

Hmmmm, I thought. *Something* is going on here . . .

CHAPTER 11

" 'B ye, Mom! 'Bye, Janine!" I called over my shoulder.

" 'Bye!" I heard them answer.

The Wilders' station wagon was parked in front of my house. Rosie was waving from the backseat. It was four-thirty on a Thursday, and they were picking me up to take me to . . .

Uncle Dandy's Star Machine!

Rosie was going to be on the show!

I know, I know. Uncle Dandy isn't exactly big-time. Still, I was really happy for Rosie. *And* I was excited to be going to a TV station.

You know what else? I was the only guest Rosie had invited, and it felt nice to be asked. As impossible as it seemed, Rosie and I were becoming friends. Since I had found out about her hidden artistic talent, she had really loosened up.

But one thing bothered me. I couldn't understand why in the world she had to keep her talent a secret. Obviously her parents had encouraged her other abilities. Why did she have to hide the one thing she liked best?

I tried not to think about that as I got in the car. Rosie and her parents seemed excited. Mrs. Wilder had asked her sister to stay with their mother for the evening, and Mr. Wilder had left work early.

"Hartford, here we come!" Mr. Wilder said. He looked back and winked at us with his dark, dark eyes. I wondered if *he* had ever wanted to be a performer.

"Now Rosie, before we get to the highway, are you sure you have everything?" Mrs. Wilder asked. "Your music? Your pitch pipe? Your tap shoes?"

"Mom," Rosie said. "I'm not *dancing*. Just singing and playing, remember?"

"Well, you never know when you might be asked to," Mrs. Wilder said. "It's always good to be prepared."

"Ginger, you're such a stage mother," Mr. Wilder said with a smile.

Mrs. Wilder laughed. "Sorry, I'm just being swept away with excitement!" Then she turned to her husband with a mischievous grin and said, "You should talk, George!"

"Mea culpa," Mr. Wilder replied, and Rosie smiled, as if she knew what that meant.

96

(Janine told me later that it means *I'm guilty* in Latin.)

The ride was fun. We played Guess the License Plate and a bunch of other car games. But when the Wilders started singing songs (in harmony), they sounded so good I just listened.

The TV station was actually outside of Hartford. It was in a pretty dull area, with squat brick buildings and parking lots full of trucks and buses. The TV station looked like every other building, except for the huge antenna on top.

We stepped into a small waiting room with a worn linoleum floor and a water cooler. Not exactly glamorous.

A woman with a beehive hairdo and a telephone headset said, "You here for the *Dandy* show?"

"Yes," Mr. Wilder replied. "This is one of the talents." He gently pushed Rosie in front of him.

"Hi, sweetie," the woman said. "Just go through the door and look for Studio Four. It'll be on your right."

"Thanks," we all said together.

Inside the door was a long, wide corridor, with dozens of cables snaking along the floor. Men and women passed by, rolling enormous video cameras. I recognized one or two local TV newscasters and boy, did they look older than they do on TV! The walls were lined with studio doors. One of them swung open and I could see the set of a game show I used to watch when I was a kid. *That* made me shiver.

I wished Stacey or Kristy were with me. We'd have looked in each other's eyes and known we were squealing inside.

Rosie didn't seem fazed at all. She was mouthing the words to her song and following her parents.

I couldn't resist saying, "You are so *calm!*" to Rosie.

She shrugged. "This is nothing compared to some of the network studios in New York."

"Here it is, girls!" Mr. Wilder called out. He opened the door marked STUDIO 4 and let us go in.

What a place. Half of the room was a madhouse. People wearing headsets were running around like crazy, muttering in low voices. At first I thought they were talking to themselves, until I realized little mikes were attached to the headsets. There were cameras standing on tripods, a camera hanging from the ceiling on a crane, cameras shoved against the wall. Along a table on the other side of the room were two coffee urns and four plates of cold cuts and breads. Uncle Dandy waved to us from a corner, where a man and a woman were combing his hair and putting makeup on his face.

The other half of the room was completely empty. It was the set for the show. In the center was a polished wooden floor. Off to the side were curtains, pulled open, and a grand piano. Hanging above the set was a huge sign that said UNCLE DANDY'S STAR MACHINE in neon lights. A few rows of folding chairs faced the set (they were for the studio audience).

"Hi, what's your talent?" someone asked.

I looked around to see a girl smiling brightly at Rosie. Her parents stood behind her, smiling brightly at her.

"Singing and piano," Rosie answered.

"I'm dancing — " the girl said.

"Introduce yourself, dear," the girl's mother interrupted.

"I'm Crystal."

"I'm Rosie." Rosie smiled tightly, then stared straight ahead.

Crystal got the message. She nodded a little, frowned a little, then walked away with her parents.

I dared to say to Rosie, "She seemed pretty nice."

Rosie shook her head. "It's important not to make small talk on the set. That kind of thing can destroy your concentration, especially before a performance."

"That's right, dear," Mrs. Wilder said, putting her hand on Rosie's shoulder.

I thought that was a little weird, but I didn't say anything.

Soon Uncle Dandy came racing across the set with a clipboard in his hand. His hair (or toupee) had so much spray in it, it looked like a helmet. "Where are all the kids?" he shouted.

"Some of them are in the green room, Mr. Beasley," a bearded guy replied from behind us.

"What are they doing there?" Uncle Dandy demanded. "We're at half hour. Get them in here!"

Then he turned to Rosie and Crystal and gave them a huge smile. "Howdy. 'Dya have a nice trip here?"

"Uh-huh," Rosie and Crystal said.

Uncle Dandy looked up to see the bearded man talking to someone. "*Now*, Bickford!" he ordered.

He kept doing that — practically barking at the adults, but using this sugar-sweet voice for kids.

When the other talents came in, he led them

all onto the set. The Wilders, the other families and friends, and I squeezed into the studio audience chairs.

We listened to Uncle Dandy's pep talk. "Wow, here we are!" he exclaimed with a goony smile, clapping his hands. "Is everybody excited?"

"Yes!" the kids screamed.

Then he put on a serious expression. "Boys and girls, this is a super-duper big day. It's our premiere show! Believe me, I know how you must feel. All these lights and cameras, everyone in Central and parts of Southern Connecticut watching . . . but I want you to know Uncle Dandy is behind you a hundred and a half percent. I want you all to have the *bestest, funnest, Uncle Dandiest* time! Remember, we're one big, happy family!"

The speech was so corny, I don't know how the kids kept from cracking up.

As Uncle Dandy spoke, beads of sweat formed on his forehead. He was smiling broadly, but his eyes were darting all around. He was making me nervous, and I wasn't even on the show! After the speech he announced the order in which the performers would appear. Rosie was going to be last, with her two songs.

"They always save the best for last," Mr. Wilder whispered to his wife and me.

101

Soon the performers were taken into a waiting room, out of sight. Ms. Yu arrived late, waved to us, and stood against the wall. The audience lights dimmed and these *huge* spotlights lit up the stage so brightly I had to squint. Then this incredibly loud, tinny-sounding music started. Uncle Dandy ran onto the stage so fast he almost fell over. "Who-o-oa! Har har — that was a close one! Well, hello out there, boys and girls! It's time for *Uncle Dandy's Star Machine*!"

He pointed to the neon lights, which flashed on and off. But two letters were dead, so when it lit up it looked like ·UNCLE ANDY'S TAR MACHINE.

Off to the side, a woman held up a sign that said WILD APPLAUSE. We all applauded loudly.

"Yes, well, we have quite a show for you today . . ." As Uncle Dandy bounced to the beat of the music, his shirt came untucked. And then I discovered he *was* wearing a toupee, because it began to slip forward on his forehead. I almost burst out laughing.

Did I ever breathe a sigh of relief when the first act began. A little girl danced to some rock music.

She was pretty good, and so were most of the other acts — a ventriloquist, a ballerina, a few singers, a tap dancer (which caused Mrs. Wilder to whisper, "She's no Rosie!" to Mr. Wilder), and a kid who walked on stilts and juggled.

When Rosie went onstage, I felt a chill race through me. My stomach churned. I looked at the Wilders. They were holding hands and smiling calmly.

As Rosie played a complicated classical song, two camera people rolled toward her. They swooped close to her face, then her hands. The camera on the crane swung above her. I don't know how she could keep concentrating.

But she didn't make one mistake. Then, after the song was over and we cheered our lungs out, she sat down again. This time she played a slow ballad from a Broadway show, *and* sang along. She never looked at her fingers. She'd sing facing one camera, then smoothly look at another. Somehow she always knew which one she was on.

I felt so proud of her!

After her number, the Wilders and I practically leaped to our feet. I shouted "Brava!" and whistled.

Uncle Dandy made some dumb closing remarks, and soon the overhead lights were turned on again. As we stood up, the performers began filing back into the studio.

There were hugs and kisses all over the place. I practically smothered Rosie. "You were *so* fantastic!" I said.

"Thanks," she replied with a smile.

"Wonderful, darling," Mr. Wilder said. "As always."

"Super!" Mrs. Wilder added.

"The best!" Ms. Yu said proudly.

We chatted for awhile. Ms. Yu left to talk to Uncle Dandy, who was wiping his face with a towel.

Soon a handsome, tanned man with moussed hair approached Rosie and said, "Let me add my congratulations to everyone else's. I'm Raymond Mendez of Mendez Teen 'n' Tiny Talent. Do you have an agent representing you theatrically?" He handed a card to Mrs. Wilder.

"Yes, I have — " Rosie began.

But her father cut her off. "I see you have an office in New York," he said.

"And we're about to open one in L.A.," Mr. Mendez added. "We specialize in juvenile talent."

"And you have movie contacts?" Mrs. Wilder asked.

"With all the studios," answered Mr. Mendez.

The conversation obviously bothered Rosie. *"Mom,"* she said, "I have a contract with Ms. Yu!"

"Yes, of course, dear," Mrs. Wilder said. "But it's always good to keep your options open. Thank you, Mr. Mendez. We'll keep your card."

When he was out of sight, Mr. Wilder said softly, "This could be an excellent career move, Rosie. Don't worry about Ms. Yu. Contracts are made to be broken."

"But Dad — " Mr. and Mrs. Wilder were pulled aside by the parents of Crystal. They didn't hear Rosie say, "I *like* Ms. Yu!"

Before long, we said good-bye to Uncle Dandy and headed out to the parking lot. As we drove off, Mr. and Mrs. Wilder launched a conversation about the pros and cons of the Mendez Teen 'n' Tiny Talent agency.

Rosie and I tuned them out in the backseat. "Rosie, you were so good I practically cried."

"Yeah?" Rosie said. "It was no big deal. You know, you rehearse it and you do it."

"How did you know which cameras to look at?" I asked.

"The one that's on is the one with the red light," she said. "It's easy."

She looked out the window at the passing shops. I was amazed. She didn't seem to want to talk about the show at all. It was as if she'd just finished some semi-interesting chore and wanted to move on to the next thing.

Suddenly Rosie cried out, "Oooh! Let's stop at that ice cream shop! Can we have a treat? I'm so-o-o-o hungry!"

Mr. Wilder smiled. "Not tonight, sweetheart. It's getting late, and you have a rehearsal with Mr. Bryan and Ms. Van Cott in the morning for your dinner-theater audition."

That's when the fireworks began.

Rosie stomped her feet and screamed, "But I want *ice cream!* I don't want to have a stupid rehearsal!"

"*Rosi-i-i-ie,*" Mrs. Wilder said. "Behave yourself. You need your sleep if you want your voice to stay in shape."

"I don't *care* about my voice! I don't *care* about dancing! I don't *care* about that dumb audition!"

"I know how you feel, darling," Mr. Wilder said. "But you're a performer, and performers have to have discipline."

"*That's not what I am!*" Rosie was shrieking now. "*I'm a kid! I just want to get ice cream like a normal kid!*"

The Wilders just fell silent and kept on driving. Rosie folded her arms and curled into a ball.

No one said a word during the rest of the trip. I felt so sad for Rosie. I tried to comfort her, but she shrank away from me. So I just stared out the window. I don't remember one thing I saw.

CHAPTER 12

Friday

Well, this isn't exactly about baby-sitting, but it's about our main topic of conversation these days — Rosie Wilder.

I was curious to meet her, and I finally did when Claudia and I went to the Grand Crossword Competition together.

You were right about her brains, Claud. She was incredible! You were also right about a few other things...

Curious? I practically had to drag Mary Anne to the Crossword Competition that Thursday. No one else could go with me. Still, Mary Anne *almost* decided to go home and do her homework.

I'm glad she came to SES. Rosie needed as much help as she could get. And I don't mean with the puzzles.

Let me start at the beginning. The Wilders couldn't go to the contest because Mrs. Wilder's mom needed to be taken to the hospital. So I was in charge. Now, Stacey had told me how the other kids treated Rosie at school, so I was determined to give her as much support as I could.

Mary Anne and I went straight to Stoneybrook Elementary after school. The contest was to be held in the auditorium. A bunch of our clients were there — Charlotte Johanssen, some of the Pike kids, Haley Braddock, Marilyn and Carolyn Arnold. We had to wave and shout "Hello" a lot.

On the stage were three enormous blackboards on wheels. Some teachers were drawing crossword puzzles onto them, carefully copying the puzzles from books. The blackboards were facing the back of the stage, so the audience (and the contestants) couldn't see the puzzles in advance.

The auditorium was fairly crowded so we sat toward the back. When Rosie came in, she ran over to us. "Hi," she said. "I'm glad you're here."

"We're your cheering section," I said. "This is my friend Mary Anne Spier."

"Hi," Mary Anne said. "I've heard all about you."

Rosie smiled. "Thanks. Well, I'm going to hang out in the back till we start. I need to stay focused."

As soon as she left, Mary Anne whispered to me, *"Stay focused?"*

I shrugged. "That's Rosie. Seven going on twenty-five."

Behind us, we heard a burst of giggling. A girl was saying, "Ew! The brain!"

We turned to see a group of girls walking past Rosie.

"She's not talking to us," another girl said. "She only talks to Uncle Dandy."

The girls giggled again, then found seats together.

Poor Rosie. I tried to catch her eye, so I could give her a thumbs-up or something. But she was pacing gloomily behind the last row, staring at the floor.

Soon Ms. Reynolds, the SES principal, walked onto the stage and announced, "Okay, let's take our seats. The competition's about to begin. Competing this evening is the winner from each grade, one of whom will become the school champ. In the fifth grade, Nicole Ficaro — "

"Ya-a-a-ay!" came a big cheer from one section of the auditorium.

"In the fourth grade," Ms. Reynolds continued, "Joseph Nicholas — "

Another huge cheer from another part of the auditorium.

"And in the third grade, Rosie Wilder!"

Well, Mary Anne and I cheered loudly. I think a couple of other kids did, too, but I wasn't sure. If they did, they were drowned out by some loud "Boo's" and giggles.

My heart sank. If I'd been Rosie and heard that, I would have been mortified.

"All right," Ms. Reynolds said sternly. "If you have a negative opinion, you are advised to keep it to yourself." She glared at the group of unruly kids, and boy, did they squirm. Then she said, "All right. I'll explain the rules. There are three puzzles, one for each grade. The higher the grade, the harder the puzzle. The contestants will have twenty minutes to complete their puzzles. At the end, the one who has filled in the most correct answers wins. There is to be no — I repeat, no — helping from the audience members. Anyone who does will be expelled from the room." She glanced around. "Okay, will the contestants please come to the stage?"

Rosie and the other two walked down the aisles. One of the girls who had taunted Rosie whispered something to her friends, and they started snickering.

I'm sure Rosie heard them, but she just kept walking.

As the three contestants stepped onstage, Ms. Reynolds gave them a warm smile and wished them good luck. Then she said, "All right, *begin!*"

The teachers turned the blackboards around and raced to the sides of the stage to bring out stools for the kids.

The three kids began scribbling away. Rosie, who was the shortest, had to step on and off her stool constantly.

Some people in the audience found that hilarious. "It's a jumping bean!" someone called out. That set off the girls, who were waiting for an excuse to laugh.

One of the teachers ran to them and angrily shushed them.

Meanwhile Rosie was doing a great job. She figured out the easy clues right away. For "President Abraham _____ " she wrote LIN-

COLN, for "Opposite of high" she wrote LOW — things like that.

But there were some really tough clues, too. "What's a 'small, furry marsupial'?" Mary Anne whispered.

"Beats me," I said. "How about the author of 'The Owl and the Pussycat' — Edward *Blank*? Edward Allan Poe?" I guessed.

"It's *Edgar* Allan Poe," Mary Anne said. "Besides, there are only four letters."

I heard an explosion of laughter, this time from a group of boys. Rosie had just filled in a word, which left the word for Ten Across looking like this:

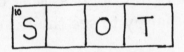

The clue was "An opening," and the answer was SLOT, of course, but you can imagine which letter the boys had pictured in the blank: an N.

"Hey, Rosie, here's a hint for Ten Across — yourself!" one of the boys called out.

This time Ms. Reynolds herself approached the boy. She took his arm and walked him out of the auditorium. As Rosie filled in the L for SLOT, another boy yelled, "Wro-o-o-ng — EHHHH," imitating an electronic buzzer.

113

Kids can be really cruel, but I think they're worse in a group situation. You know how it is, one person starts and everyone has to copy. Mary Anne and I were *so* angry, but there was nothing we could do.

Anyway, Rosie just kept writing and writing, with that same grim expression she wore when she played the piano. She figured out the furry marsupial (KOALA) and the "Owl and the Pussycat" author (LEAR).

With about one and a half minutes left, she filled in her last letter, slammed down the chalk, and called out, "Finished!"

There were a few groans from the crowd, but a few cheers, too. I guess *some* of the third-graders were happy to see their classmate finish first.

Rosie waited by the blackboard until the buzzer went off. Both Joseph and Nicole quickly filled in all their boxes in the nick of time.

The teachers stood in front of the blackboards and checked the answers. They mumbled to themselves, then mumbled to Ms. Reynolds.

Ms. Reynolds nodded. She stepped to the front of the stage. "Let's have a big hand for the new Stoneybrook Elementary School Crossword Champ — Rosie Wilder!"

Mary Anne and I jumped up and cheered. We didn't care what the other kids thought. Ms. Reynolds gave Rosie a trophy and a hug, which was good for one or two cries of "Ew" from the audience.

Rosie took the trophy and slunk off the stage. We ran to her.

"Congratulations!" I said. "I knew you'd do it!"

"You were amazing!" added Mary Anne. "I didn't know half those clues."

All Rosie said was, "Can we go now?"

We walked outside with her and headed away from the school. Rosie was silent for awhile, staring straight ahead and clutching her trophy. Then she said, "Why do they do that?"

"You mean, those kids?" I asked gently.

Rosie nodded. "They *always* treat me like that. I don't know why. I never do anything bad to them. I just try to do my best, that's all. And they gang up on me and tease me and call me names. I mean, even the third-graders didn't cheer for me."

Rosie began to cry. She was clutching her trophy so hard her knuckles had turned white.

Mary Anne and I put our arms around her. "Oh, Rosie, it's okay," I said. "It isn't easy being different from everybody. People have a hard time understanding you."

"That's right," Mary Anne said. "Look at the problems Claudia has."

Rosie sniffed and brushed back her tears. "C-Claudia?" She looked at me like a wounded puppy. "But you're so popular!"

I smiled. "Well, maybe. But in my family, I'm the only one who isn't a brain. You met my sister, right? I love her, but can you imagine growing up with *her* for a sister? My parents always compared me to her, but I could never do as well in school as she does. Not in a million years! I felt like a freak. No one in my family is *anything* like me."

"But didn't your parents *see* what a great artist you were?" Rosie asked.

"Well, now they do, sort of," I said. "But I'm thirteen. It's taken a long time."

We talked all the way to Rosie's house. When we neared Burnt Hill Road, Mary Anne said, "I have to go home this way." She smiled warmly at Rosie. "I barely know you, Rosie, but I think you're very special, even aside from your talents."

You should have seen Rosie beam.

By the time Rosie and I reached her house, she was feeling a little better. We went inside and each ate a big helping of potato salad from the refrigerator.

I checked the note Mrs. Wilder had left,

which said she and Mr. Wilder would be back in time for Rosie's five-thirty voice lesson. It was only four forty-five, so I said to Rosie, "Well, what do you want to do? Get ready for your lesson?"

Rosie grinned slyly. "I want to *draw!*"

"I *knew* you were going to say that!" I said. I found my backpack and pulled out my drawing supplies.

Rosie ran upstairs and came down with a fistful of her own sketches and a paper shopping bag. "I drew a Life Saver and a peppermint stick," she said, "but then I tried drawing a Doritos bag, and it ended up looking like a potato sack . . ."

She showed me what she'd done. Then she pulled her subjects out of the shopping bag and set them on the table.

We started with the Life Saver. I explained what she could do to make the shading better and smooth the lines.

We worked hard, going from drawing to drawing. We erased, improved, experimented. Some of the results were good, but some were hilariously awful. At one point, when Rosie was working on the crinkled outline of a Doritos bag, she drew what looked like the outline of a dog. We cracked up. "Arf! Arf!" I barked.

"Ow-oooo!" Rosie howled.

I began to sniff like a dog, moving my head left and right.

And that's when I saw Mr. and Mrs. Wilder. They were standing in the kitchen doorway, staring at us as if we'd lost our minds.

CHAPTER 13

"Mom, Dad," Rosie said. "I didn't hear you come in."

"You were . . . barking too loudly," Mr. Wilder said. He smiled, but he obviously was *not* amused.

"Did Ms. Van Cott call in sick?" Mrs. Wilder asked.

"No," Rosie said, hanging her head.

"Then why aren't you practicing for your lesson?"

"And isn't tomorrow the due date for your math project?" Mr. Wilder asked.

Instead of answering, Rosie reached for her trophy. Her face brightened as she held it out to her parents. "Look, I won the Grand Crossword Competition!"

"*Terrific*, sweetheart!" Mr. Wilder said with a big grin. He took the trophy and admired it in the overhead light. "I'm going to put this front and center in the trophy case."

Mrs. Wilder bent down and kissed her daughter on the cheek. "I'm so proud of you, Rosie."

"Thanks," Rosie said.

But Mrs. Wilder had caught a close-up glimpse of Rosie's drawing. "What is that, dear?" she asked, frowning at it.

"A bag of Doritos," Rosie said meekly.

"A bag of Doritos," Mrs. Wilder repeated. "Did *you* draw that?"

"Mm-hm," answered Rosie.

"You, uh, don't have anything better to do with your time?" asked her father.

"I finished my math project already," said Rosie quickly.

Mr. Wilder nodded. "Very good. And did you practice for your lesson, too?"

"No, but — "

"Really, Rosie, I'm surprised at you," Mrs. Wilder said. "Drawing a bag of chips when your teacher is about to arrive."

"But Claudia's teaching me how to — " Rosie protested.

"Honey," Mr. Wilder said, "we're not spending our hard-earned money on your career just so you can fritter away your time — "

"I'm not *frittering!*" Rosie shouted. "I don't *want* to practice!"

"Rosie," Mr. Wilder said, "let's not have a

replay of the night we came back from the Uncle Dandy show."

"I *hate* Uncle Dandy!" Rosie snapped. "He's stupid and ugly, and if he invites me back, I'm going to turn him down!"

"Fine," Mr. Wilder said with a sigh. "I realize you were in another league from the other talents, but the show served its purpose. Now it's over. But that doesn't mean we can let up. Life moves on. There's your audition, your commercial booking next week — "

Rosie slammed her hand on the table. "I don't *care* about some dumb musical! And I'm *tired* of going into New York! I hate my life! I *never* have any fun except when Claudia comes over! All I do is work, work, work. And I'm not going to do it *anymore!*"

With that, Rosie slid out of her chair, stomped upstairs, and slammed her door shut.

"*Rosie!*" Mr. Wilder called after her. "Mary Rose, you come down here *right now!*"

"No!" Rosie yelled back, her voice choked with tears.

"Leave her, George," Mrs. Wilder said. "She needs to be alone for a few minutes."

Rosie's parents looked a little shaky. I gathered Rosie didn't act like that too often. The Wilders kind of stood there, staring at the space between themselves and me.

As for me? Well, I wanted to *die*. I felt as if I had taken their little girl and created a monster. At least, I was sure that was the way *they* saw the situation.

I thought about slipping out the back door, but then realized I hadn't done anything wrong.

I took a deep, deep breath. The Wilders looked at me. For a second I thought they were going to throw me out of the house. But they didn't say a word, which just made things worse. So I decided to break the silence.

"Auungh . . ."

Great beginning, Claudia.

My mouth was so dry I couldn't even say "Uh . . ." I swallowed and tried again. "Mr. and Mrs. Wilder, I've done a lot of baby-sitting, and I've never met anyone as gifted as your daughter. She's in a class by herself."

I looked from one to the other. I hoped that flattering Rosie would soften them a little, but it didn't seem to. I was just telling them what they already knew.

I had to tell them what they *didn't* know.

"I know how close you are to Rosie, and what an active part you take in her interests," I said. "But, believe it or not, I think I've found another incredible talent in your daughter. And she's hiding it."

"What do you mean?" Mr. Wilder asked.

"Well, I think Rosie is a really gifted artist," I said.

Mrs. Wilder sighed. "She *doodles*. That's all. She's never shown any serious interest in art."

"You haven't seen the projects she works on in her room." I spread out the sketches she had brought down. "Do you think many seven-year-olds can draw like this?"

Mr. Wilder squinted and bent down. "These are good?"

"Look at this." I showed him the Life Saver drawing. "Most kids Rosie's age would draw two circles, one inside the other. But she already knows how to use shadowing and create perspective. It looks three-dimensional. Those are things you usually have to learn from teachers. I know. I've taken tons of lessons myself."

"Oh?" Mrs. Wilder said. She looked a little suspicious.

"I've studied in school and at the Stoneybrook Arts Center; I've also studied in New York City with a great teacher named McKenzie Clarke. I'm not saying that to brag, but — "

"No, that's fine," Mr. Wilder said. "I've heard of McKenzie Clarke. Go on."

"Well, I know plenty of kids, even kids my own age in the class in New York, who don't have Rosie's potential. I know this may seem silly, but look at the proportions of the Doritos bag she drew. I mean, they're not perfect, but do you know how hard it is to get them right? And take a look at this peppermint stick . . ."

The Wilders looked closely at the drawings. I could tell they were interested. But I could also see that old light bulb switching on over their heads.

"Maybe we should contact McKenzie Clarke," Mrs. Wilder said. "On our trips to New York we could pop up to his studio."

"Or maybe he holds a Saturday afternoon class," Mr. Wilder went on.

Ugh. Just what I was afraid of. Now the Wilders saw yet another career path for their daughter. They were going to squeeze Rosie's love for art out of her, just like they had done with dance and music and singing.

Suddenly everything became clear to me. *That* was why Rosie kept her art a secret. She knew her parents would push her too hard. Art was something she could enjoy on her own.

"The thing is," I said, "she really *loves* art. You should see her face light up!" (I almost compared it to the glum look she wore while doing everything else, but that would have been going *too* far.)

"Isn't that something," Mrs. Wilder said.

An idea hit me — a *fun* way to involve Rosie

in her drawing. "You know, I'm having an art show on Saturday," I said. "Just in my garage, that's all, for friends and neighbors and family. If you don't mind, I'd like to ask Rosie to show some of her drawings at the opening."

I didn't mention the theme was junk food. Somehow I didn't think the Wilders would like that idea.

"Sounds fine to me," Mr. Wilder said, "in *theory*. The problem is, she has a go-see for that department store in Stamford Saturday afternoon."

"Go-see?" I repeated.

"That's what you call an audition for a modeling job."

"But that's okay," I said. "Rosie can come to the show in the morning. She doesn't have to be there the whole time. I just figured it would be a fun way for her work to get some exposure."

I think I had said exactly the right thing. Mr. Wilder nodded thoughtfully and said, "Okay by me." He looked at his wife. "Ginger?"

"Well, I suppose," she said. "As long as it doesn't interfere with her other activities."

"Great!" I exclaimed. "I'll go ask Rosie."

I took the stairs two at a time, then knocked on her door. "Rosie?"

"Come in," Rosie muttered.

I pushed the door open. Rosie was at her desk, drawing quietly.

She looked up and said, "They told you never to come back, right?"

I sat down on her bed. "Nope. As a matter of fact, I talked them into letting you show your drawings at my opening. If you want to, that is."

Rosie stared at me, dumbfounded.

"Well?" I asked.

"You're not joking, are you?" she said.

I shook my head. "No joke. Do you want to?"

Rosie's frown faded. A smile crept across her face. Then she jumped out of her chair and screamed. "*Do* I? Yes!"

"Great!" I said. "You better get to work polishing up those sketches."

"I will!" Rosie said excitedly. "Oh, I can't wait. Thank you, Claudia!"

Just then the doorbell rang. Rosie's smile melted away. "That's Ms. Van Cott," she said, plopping back into her chair.

"Well, it's time for me to go, anyway," I said. "I'll call you tomorrow."

Rosie let out a big sigh. "Ohhh . . . how am I going to have *time* to prepare for the show, Claudia? I have all these stupid lessons and clubs, and the audition and the go-see . . ."

"You'll manage, Rosie," I said. "I have faith in you. But there's one thing I want you to promise me."

"What?"

"Sometime soon you should have a talk with your parents. Let them know exactly what kinds of things you want to do and don't want to do. Okay?"

Rosie smiled and nodded. "Okay."

I gave her a big hug, and then we scooted down the stairs.

CHAPTER 14

Saturday was the debut of "Claudia Lynn Kishi's 'Disposable Comestibles,' a Pop-Art Multi-Media Extravaganza."

Yes, I changed the name. *Comestibles* is another word for food. Actually, it was Janine's idea, in a way. She passed my room one night while I was arranging a bunch of junk food, and said, "Are you painting your disposable comestibles?" Well, I thought that was hilarious. I adopted the name immediately. Janine, of course, didn't quite see the humor in it.

Neither did Dawn. She thought it sounded like I was trying too hard to sound smart. But they were both missing the point. Here was this huge, complicated name that would give people the idea that they were seeing something really serious, and then the subject of the show would turn out to be junk food.

The way I saw it, one of the main things

about pop art was humor. Well, anyway, I liked the idea. I also liked the fact that we were going to have a refreshment table, serving . . . junk food! (That was my idea, too.)

The garage looked *great*. My friends and I had worked hard to clean it out, even scrubbing the cement floor. My dad was thrilled, to say the least. His first comment was, "You know, I have enough room for a little wood shop out here!"

Of course, *my* first thought was how many shows I could have in there. I could put one on annually, or one each season.

As my fellow BSC members scrambled about, doing last-minute things, Rosie adjusted and readjusted *her* sketches. Then she studied them and adjusted them *again*.

"They look perfect, Rosie," I said.

Rosie put her hand on her chin and squinted at the drawings. "Yeah? You think so?"

"If you move them one more time, the nails will come out of the wall!"

"Okay, Claudia," she said with a smile. "I'll leave them alone."

I checked the little price stickers on my paintings. I had decided not only to show them, but to try to sell them. After all, that's what artists are *supposed* to do in art galleries.

I figured I might as well get used to selling my work, since that's what I'll be doing for a living someday.

Besides, I could use the money to buy really good supplies. Or, of course, donate some of it to the Baby-sitters Club treasury.

But just *some*.

I walked outside, where Kristy and Mary Anne were tying a big sign around one of our trees:

YES, IT'S HERE!
"DISPOSABLE COMESTIBLES"
WORKS BY CLAUDIA LYNN KISHI
AND MARY ROSE WILDER
IN THE KISHI GARAGE
10:00 A.M. — 5:30 P.M.

"How are we doing?" I asked.

"We're right on schedule," Kristy said, looking at her watch. "It's nine-fifty. People will be showing up any minute."

It shouldn't surprise you to know that the Wilders were the first to arrive. They even took three photos of the *sign*, because Rosie's name was on it!

Everyone greeted the Wilders in the garage.

130

Stacey sold them each a bag of chips. Rosie was glowing with excitement.

It turned out I didn't need to worry about the Wilders not liking the junk-food concept. They seemed fascinated, looking closely at every painting. At one point, as Rosie and I were following her dad around, he said, "You know, this really *is* quite good, Rosie."

The problem was, he was pointing at the lollipop painting *I* had done. "Uh, thank you, Mr. Wilder," I said. "I painted that."

He laughed. "Oh! Well, I guess you've influenced my daughter's style so much I can't tell the drawings apart," he said. "She's catching up to you, you know, Claudia," he added with a wink.

Rosie and I gave each other a Look, then started giggling. I had figured her dad would say something competitive, but we didn't mind.

Before too long, the Papadakises showed up, and then the Barretts. Most people liked the paintings, especially the parents. Some of the kids couldn't see the point.

Things went smoothly until about twelve-thirty. That was when Alan Gray, the goon of Stoneybrook Middle School, decided to show up. He looked like (a) he had just woken up and (b) he had forgotten to take his human-being pills that morning. He couldn't stop laughing at the paintings.

"Hey, Claudia," he called out, "I see a lot of ads, but where's the art?"

"Oh, Alan, you are so funny I forgot to laugh," I said. (What a dumb expression, but Alan's the kind of guy you say things like that to.)

Fortunately my attention was taken away from Alan by a guy in a tweed coat who tapped me on my shoulder and said, "Are you Ms. Kishi?"

"Yes," I answered.

"Well, I was wandering by and saw your sign, and I must say your work has an indescribable simplicity and taste. Truly an example of form following function, rather in the style spawned from the era that brought us the Bauhaus and the dadaists."

"Uh, right," I said. Suddenly I wished I hadn't changed the name to "Disposable Comestibles." It was attracting people who really talked like that. "Thank you," I said, trying to remember what he said so I could ask Janine to translate later. "I've got to go now."

(I later found out that what he said made no sense anyway. Oh, well, at least he liked the paintings.)

I stood by the door for awhile, greeting the Pikes when they came in (which really made

132

the garage feel crowded), and then Kristy's family.

That was when I heard Suzi Barrett call out, "Yucchh! I don't like *that* one!"

I thought she saw a painting of some candy she didn't like. But when I turned around, I saw she was staring at a crude drawing of a dead cat next to a candy wrapper.

"What is *that?*" I said.

I walked toward it, and saw another wrinkled sheet of paper tacked up nearby. That one showed a terrible drawing of a grungy-looking toothless man eating a candy bar. He was smiling happily and saying "Mmm!" while the candy was flaking down his chin.

I quickly tore down the disgusting drawings. Who could have —

Then I saw Alan Gray squatting in a corner with a pad of paper and a pencil. "Hey! Cut that out!" I yelled.

Alan sprang to his feet, giving me his dumbest grin. "Go home, Alan, okay?" I said. "Don't ruin my show."

"Sure, Claudia," he said. "No problem. See you."

That was easy — *too* easy. A few minutes later, I found out why.

I saw the man in the tweed suit limping toward the garage door. He was holding one of his penny loafers and mumbling angrily.

When he saw me he held up his shoe and said, "Really! Is this considered environmental art? I don't find it amusing or appropriate."

A wad of gum was stuck to the bottom of his shoe.

"Ew!" cried Hannie Papadakis. "Gum!"

I saw her lifting her foot — which was attached to the floor by a long, pink string of chewing gum.

The same thing happened to Mrs. Barrett and Jessi. Pieces of gum were all over the floor, like little land mines.

I put the BSC members on "Alan Gray Alert," and we went around picking up the remaining pieces. Kristy whispered to me, "On Monday our first item of business will be plotting revenge!"

We weathered that crisis. The rest of the day passed uneventfully. A lot of people came to the show, and I had fun answering questions about the work. But here's the really exciting part:

By one o'clock, two people had actually bought paintings! One of those people was Ms. Besser, a teacher at SES who once helped us set up a huge sleepover at the school. The other person was Watson Brewer.

It was right around then that Rosie said to me, "We have to go to Stamford now."

"Oh, okay. Well, I think everything's under

control," I replied. "People are really enjoying your work."

"Yeah," Rosie said with a smile. "Thanks, Claudia. This was fun."

She turned to leave, but I gently took her arm. "Just a second," I said. I pulled her into a secluded corner. "Rosie, have you spoken to your parents yet — about what we discussed?"

"No," Rosie said, looking away from me. "But I will, soon."

"Promise?"

"Promise."

We said good-bye, and she left. I had Rosie's promise, and I wanted to be patient with her. But I knew the talk would be difficult for her.

I wasn't totally convinced she would find the courage to stand up to her parents.

CHAPTER 15

The following Friday was my last regular sitting job for Rosie Wilder. Mrs. Wilder's mom was recovering nicely and wasn't going to need daily care anymore.

A couple of weeks earlier I had been looking forward to this day more than my birthday and Christmas combined. But now that it had arrived, I felt sad.

The day was cloudy and drizzly. I walked Rosie home from school after her science club meeting. I could tell she felt sad, too.

We didn't say much at first. Then Rosie perked up. "Oh!" she blurted out. "The dinner theater called my mom yesterday."

From the brightness in her eyes, I knew what she was going to say — she had gotten the part.

"I was rejected," she said.

At first I thought she was joking. I smiled. "Yeah, sure."

"No, I mean it," Rosie insisted. "It wasn't because of my audition, they said. It was because they wanted a girl with darker features to look like the actress playing the mother."

"Oh, Rosie," I said. "I'm so sorry."

"I'm not," Rosie replied with a shrug. "Well, maybe just a little, but not much."

"Really?" I couldn't believe my ears. "Why not?"

"I don't know. The part was sort of dumb, and it would have meant going to the theater every night, *and* weekends. And when would I have had time to draw?" She looked up and gave me this humongous grin.

"Now you're talking!" I said.

"Claudia, can we do fun stuff when we get home? I hardly have any homework, and it's your last day."

"Sure," I said.

I thought of a perfect project, but I wouldn't tell Rosie the details right away. Instead, I made her do some errands with me. First we raided the Wilders' basement for old magazines and brought them up to the kitchen. Then we cut out cartoon figures, and pictures of people and animals. They had to be upright, not lying down or on all fours. They also had to be approximately the same size, and the more unusual-looking the better.

When we had found about twenty pictures, Rosie said, "Okay, now what?"

"Now we need glue," I answered.

Rosie ran and got some. "Claudia, tell me what we're doing!"

"Now we have to cut each of these figures into three pieces — the head, the body, and the legs. Okay?"

Rosie's eyes lit up. "And then mix and match them, right?"

"Right!"

We got to work. I made a creature with the feet of a penguin, the belly of a grizzly bear, and the head of Fred Flintstone.

Rosie's first try was the head of a horse, the body of a man in a suit, and the legs of a baby from a diaper ad.

When we got tired of the cutouts we began drawing our own strange creatures. Soon we were howling with laughter.

Then we played hangman for awhile. We used a dictionary and found the biggest words possible. That way we could draw the most complicated hangmen you ever saw — toes, fingers, warts, glasses, backpacks, you name it. They were masterpieces!

It was a great afternoon.

Around six-thirty the weather cleared, and

an amazing sunset was beginning. "Let's take a walk," I suggested.

We strolled along Elm Street, breathing the cool air deeply. When we turned up Locust Avenue, Rosie said, "You know, Claudia, I finally did it."

"Did what?" I asked.

"Had the talk with my parents."

"Really?" I hadn't wanted to ask, because I didn't feel like pushing her. But boy, was I relieved. "Well, what happened?"

"First I told them I liked *some* of my activities," answered Rosie, "but not all of them. Also, I told them I was doing too many things. 'And you know,' I said, 'when you do too much, you start to hate everything.' "

"That's fantastic, Rosie. It must have been hard to tell them that! What did they say?"

"I was *so-o-o* surprised. They didn't even yell at me. They kind of nodded. Then my mom asked what I wanted to do, and I told her I just needed more free time. I wanted to concentrate on the things I like."

"And they agreed?"

"Well, they didn't seem *too* unhappy. Dad asked what things I wanted to do. And I had thought about it the whole week long, so I knew what to say. I told him I wanted to do one school thing, one performance thing, and one creative thing. And so I picked out my favorites — math club, violin, and art classes."

"Art classes?" I said. "But you've never taken any."

"I know," Rosie replied. "I want to start."

"Will your parents let you?"

"I'm still not sure. They said they'd talk things over with Ms. Yu. But I overheard my dad mention to my mom that there was this great art-supply store near where he works."

"That's a good sign," I said.

"Yeah. And if they say yes, I know the perfect art teacher." Rosie looked up at me with a hopeful grin.

"You mean — but I never — " I wasn't expecting her to say that, but it sounded like a fun idea. "Well, okay, it's a deal!"

"Yea!" Rosie exclaimed. "Thanks, teach."

"Oh, by the way," I said. "I forgot to tell you. I sold a third painting — *Milk Duds, Spilled.*"

"Yeah? Who bought it?"

"Janine."

"Janine?" Rosie repeated. "That's nice. I always liked her."

She caught my glance, and we both laughed. Then we headed back to the Wilder house, skipping all the way.

About the Author

ANN M. MARTIN did *a lot* of baby-sitting when she was growing up in Princeton, New Jersey. She is a former editor of books for children, and was graduated from Smith College.

Ms. Martin lives in New York City with her cats, Mouse and Rosie. She likes ice cream and *I Love Lucy*; and she hates to cook.

Look for #50

DAWN'S BIG DATE

"There he is!" Logan cried suddenly.

A boy with short, wavy, dark hair came out the doorway along with the other arriving passengers. Lewis had told me in a letter that he was five feet ten inches, but he looked taller. He was thin but not skinny. And a lot handsomer than he looked in his picture.

In a moment he spotted us. His face broke into this absolutely great smile — even better than the smile in his picture.

I'm not sure what love at first sight feels like. But I think that's what I felt right then. Lewis was even better than I expected. Mary Anne had been right, too. He had a great voice.

"Hi! hi," he said, as he hugged his aunt and uncle. He and Logan hugged, then they punched each other on the arms a little. "Man! I'm glad to see you!" Lewis told Logan.

"Me, too!" said Logan. "We are going to

have a blast." Logan stood there smiling, then he remembered Mary Anne and me. "This is Mary Anne. And this is Dawn."

"Hi," I said a little shyly.

"Dawn, hi," said Lewis. He didn't give me his big, gorgeous smile. His mouth kind of quivered up into a small shaky one. "We meet at last."

Read all the books
in the Baby-sitters Club series
by Ann M. Martin